in 1931 and m... ...en his father became ... Lithuanian Government-in-E... ...blishing in the early 1950s, becoming ... Editor with Galaxy Publications and later ...ditorial Director of Playboy Press. He sold his first work of fiction in 1952 and his short stories began to appear in magazines such as *Astounding* and *Infinity* as well as in *Galaxy* (the best of these are gathered in *The Unexpected Dimension*, *Budrys' Inferno* and *Blood and Burning*). His novels include *Who?* (1958), *Rogue Moon* (1960) and *Michaelmas* (1977).

By the same author in Fontana

Who?
Rogue Moon
The Unexpected Dimension
Michaelmas

The Iron Thorn

Algis Budrys

Fontana/Collins

First published in Great Britain by
Victor Gollancz, 1968
First issued in Fontana 1980

Made and printed in Great Britain by
William Collins Sons & Co Ltd, Glasgow

This is for Geoff, who told me why it was possible,
and for Barbara who told me how it ended.

Chapter One

I

The floor of the world was rippled like the bottom of an ocean. The setting sun inked each ripple with violet shadow. Striped and dappled, the low dunes lay piled one beyond the other like stiff people in blankets filling the world to its edges.

Those edges stood high and cruel. The eastern horizon was a blue-black wall below a flaring shallow arc of eaten rust whose ends sank out of sight far to the left and right. Occasional nearer masses of rock glowed, their sunward faces orange, pitted and bright against the featureless shadow under the rusty edge. Above that horizon, tiny flecks of unwavering light were stabbing themselves through the black windings of Creation.

Towards that horizon the Amsir sped, its clawed, wide-toed feet thumping and hissing among the ripples as they kicked up momentary bursts of coarse sand that fell flat quickly. Each time it topped a dune, the Amsir emerged from thickening shadow and, like the rocks, glowed briefly, before, unlike the rocks, it cavorted down out of sight to pop up again on the next rise. The Amsir was half a dozen feet tall. It gripped a metal-shafted javelin across its chest with the little hands that grew halfway down the main bones of its wings.

Honor White Jackson was honning it and had a different opinion, but the Amsir was beautiful. Its beaked face was all angles and slits, like a knight's visor, and it had its great, translucent, flightless wings extended for balance. Graceful as a goblin bride, it curvetted in a flutter of lacy pennons growing from the horn of its puffed-up body and its spindled lower limbs. These made good insulation for Amsirs at rest, and were also quite useful to the humans of the Iron Thorn. Their effect now was to make a shy wonder of the beast – a pale, tossing creature that soared on in skittish, possibly joyous, quick steps.

The wings, spanning twelve-odd feet from nail-hard tip to tip, glowed pale coral in the waning sunlight and were excellent for infuriatingly shrewd changes in direction. Many times as he ran after it White Jackson had changed over to his casting stride, the brutal glass-headed dart nocked in the socket of his Amsir-bone throwing stick. Just as often the Amsir had tossed up one shoulder in a motion fraught with disdain, pivoted around the resistance of the fifteen square feet of braking surface, and been off again on a slightly altered tack. Behind the slitted, round turrets of horn in which its eyes were veiled, glittering pupils twinkled back over its shoulders.

As they traced their paired wakes of magenta dust over the great desert White Jackson and the Amsir together made a certain beauty greater than their individual own. Jackson was thinnish, long-limbed, tall and burned brown. You would never have known he came of people who had evolved to swing from limb to limb and never hold their backs quite straight. Like the Amsir, he had a lean face and glittering eyes. Like the Amsir, he ran daintily, touching the surface just long enough to gain traction for his next stride, striving never to come down flat-footed. He wore a very old bright metal cap with a pointed spike and a new chinstrap made of Amsir lace. He had a half pint of water in an Amsir-bubble strapped to the small of his back, and carried his spare dart in his left armpit. As wiry and as taut as the Amsir was ethereal to the eye, he was very much aware that this whole scene depended on a suspicious sloth in the quarry just as much as it did on the Honor's energy.

White Jackson was also aware that the Amsir's exasperating jigs and jogs had a common baseline that was leading him steadily away from the safety of the Iron Thorn. The damned bird was trying to lure him. White Jackson was new to being a Honor and if this was the sort of thing he could expect to have happening in his chosen way of life, he wanted very much to investigate it while he was still young enough to learn. Accordingly, though he now and then came down on his soles in the jolting, slower bounds designed to transfer momentum to his poised throwing stick, he expected nothing more for his pains that what he got – a series of sharp nudges of his cap's rim against his scalp. He saw no reason to doubt that he was tougher and smarter than any Amsir or man in the world. If he wasn't, now was none too soon to learn it. He was content to keep running all day – barring one limitation he couldn't help – and he expected the Amsir would spring its trap whenever it was dark enough for it. He was even willing to help spring it, if the trap was what he suspected it was.

As they ran on, playing their charade on each other, the Amsir undoubtedly had its own motives for being where it was. Meanwhile, Jackson was thinking that if he brought in the Amsir, his brother, Black, would treat him one way, and another if he did not. Though his brother was always very good to him. He was thinking that it would be pleasant to sit down to the community table with the demeanour of one who has killed what is being eaten. He imagined this would have its effect on women, and might go some distance towards getting elders off his back. But all this was coloured by the simple joy of being tirelessly strong and a Honor in a world bounded by sand and Amsirs, populated mostly by dull farmers, and centred on the Thorn to which the farmers clung.

He looked back over his shoulder to locate the Thorn. He had got very far away from it. Only the top several dozen feet of its black silhouette were visible over the horizon. There was no doubt that if he lost his cap now, there would be a few very bad moments of death for him and damned little else. What puzzled him was that the Amsir was not giving him enough credit for intelligence.

Honor White Jackson, even more than the wise old farmers who knew better than to want anything off beyond the fields, had a clear understanding that it was bad to get out of sight of the Thorn. It was also bad to go beyond the perimeter of the fields without a cap. The proposition about the cap had been proved to him by his brother, who had taken him to the desert and pulled his cap off. The air around White Jackson had instantly turned into thirsty burning ice. The sun had become a pale, cold hammer that left his skin itchy for hours after the cap was clapped back on his head, and would have blackened his frozen corpse given the chance. The proposition about never getting out of sight of the Thorn, cap or no, Jackson took on faith in Black's word as an established professional Honor. There were also the elders, of course, who knew so bloody much that only their constant open-mouthedness prevented its running out their ears. And there were the elders' women, whose job in life seemed to lie in giving girls all sorts of useful tips on how tricky life was.

With all this information being passed around the humans since time began with the creation of the Thorn, it was inconceivable that the Amsirs hadn't deduced how much of it was true and how much of it the humans believed enough to act on. The Amsirs after all had been in the desert beyond the fields since time began, and had seen many a farmer turn his plough, and many a Honor popping up from his night-laid ambush in a dune.

The story was that the world hadn't been made for Amsirs; Amsirs had been made for the world. Either way, it was surely no world for men, and men could be presumed to know it. Therefore, thought White Jackson as he skimmed across the sand, with faint swirls in the space immediately around him, as if the air were nearly-boiling water, what was the Amsir's plan? Did it honestly expect him to follow it over the Thorn's horizon and drop dead for its benefit?

That seemed to be the idea.

It really did. Having seen a Amsir get away from an ambush and carefully maintain half-speed with all the appearance of going full out, White Jackson was prepared to believe there was more to honning Amsirs than had ever been spelled out for him. A while ago, the beast had started working him around behind one of the rare rock outcroppings, and Jackson had been ready to expect three or four more Amsirs, waiting to jump him. But nothing like that was happening; the shallow curve of their course was now far beyond the spongy up-thrust of bloody orange rock, and just beginning to turn in behind it. Their distance from the rock gave him a clear field to see that he and the treacherous bird were the only two live things working here.

All right. They were about as far from the Thorn as Honor White Jackson cared to go. He was going to have to night-walk back to the Thorn, solving the navigation problem by reversing his memories of every change in direction and every stage of distance he had covered since leaving it. He was, hopefully, going to have to do it with the Amsir's eighty pounds across his shoulders, and he was about ready to start. In another eight strides, he was going to stumble, lose his stick and dart, paw at his face and try to crawl back along his track, for all the world as if the Amsir had lured him over the horizon. If the bird didn't go for it, that was just too bad. If he did, he was due for Jackson's spare dart right in the throat.

But it was only three strides before the world was cold and his throat was full of splinters. He had been moving forward at a pace that covered twelve feet per second, comfortable and planning ahead, and now he was flailing forward, incapable of stopping until he fell, or of doing anything but trying to squeeze breath out of the breathless air. He thought his eyeballs would freeze. He searched indignantly for the sight of the Thorn and he couldn't understand why, if you were still inside the Thorn's horizon, an outcropping of red rock between you and it was the same as losing your cap. Black Jackson had never said a word about that, and neither had anyone else.

And now that damned Amsir was turning around.

II

The Amsir came in like fury; nothing in the world moved faster than one of its kind when it wanted to, and it wanted Honor White Jackson very soon. Its wings were flung up like a hook for each moon. The javelin was caught halfway up its shaft in the bereft little right hand that grew where the wing folded in mid-span, thumb and all three fingers making a bony fist. The Amsir was gathering speed as it ran, and its strides were growing longer and more urgent. It was almost as near to flying as it could get. The wings were folding into leathery cups for the thin air, and beating with a rattling thrum that raised wakes of dust beside its springing knees. Now White Jackson could see its full face – the delighted grin of its beak, the adrenalin-exaltation of its eyes. Its talons chuckled through the sand.

Jackson almost didn't care. He knew what was doing it to him – it was the cold and the choking that were making him all concerned with what went on inside. After Black had shown him the trick with the cap, he had thought for a long time about what had happened, and although several old women had told him it was a kind of sunstroke and perhaps impiety's simple reward, he had decided it was cold and lack of air. Sudden lack of air, that caught a man halfway through drawing a breath, and made his heart nearly stop with fear when an everyday useful action suddenly got him nothing but savage disappointment. So he could understand why his body wanted to double over on itself and his hands wanted to beat on his throat.

He had tried it out, getting one of the neighbour kids to hit him in the stomach, and it had been a feeling a lot like that – no cold or burning in the eyes and nose, but the same helplessness until the spasm had passed and he could begin to pant. He guessed if he thought about it long enough, he could reason it out about the cold, too, and the thing that made bloody cracks inside his nostrils. But the Amsir was coming on. White Jackson's stick and dart were lying away on the sand just as if he'd thrown them deliberately, and he was dying.

In spite of all reasoning, he would have been helpless if he hadn't already been planning to fake this same thing. He had no air – no air at all, and you can't go long with not trying to breathe if your lungs are empty, even if you know there's no air around you any more. But he had that other dart, and as he folded he got a hand up to his armpit with a very natural motion. The Amsir had reached him. It was up in the air, at the height of a great leap, bucket-winged, and he couldn't understand why it wasn't flirting those feet like knived clubs, ready to shred him up as it came down. He would have been. But it was up there, falling at him from a height equal to its own length. Now the ends of the wings were tucked down and back, and the hand with the javelin was bent towards him. The gleaming metal point was going to hit the sand right in front of his eyes, and the Amsir shrieked, 'Yield! Yield!'

White Jackson only looked as if he was all in a heap on his knees and chest, with his face in the sand and his eyes rolling up sideways. He had the dart in the hand under his body, point sticking out of the bottom of his fist for more punch. 'Yield, wet devil!' the Amsir shrieked while Jackson got his open hand on its ankle, which was hard like a cockroach.

There was a lot of noise and flurrying, and Jackson had the Amsir down on the sand at his level. He jerked himself across the body, which was hard the same way, and wrapped in flapping stuff, and he was himself wrapped in wings and fingernails, with his head down between his shoulders as far as it could go, with the beak carving him. It was *punch* through the side of the Amsir's throat and through the spinal cord, and a feeling like a stick coming back out through a jabbed parchment window, and then, for the life of him, *punch* through the Amsir's chest and into a bubble – one of the two big, main ones down inside there under all that horn and stuff – and hug the Amsir with all the affection in the world, mouth to the chest-hole, and breathe in, in.

The Amsir flopped and flailed, wings drumming, legs dancing, back arching, but White Jackson stayed with it. The stuff coming out of the Amsir was hot with life and puffed like hollering; when his lungs were bursting full of it, he had to lock his throat against its pressure. Nor could he move his head, for his mouth was the only stopper he had to save it with.

He didn't have to breathe; he didn't have to breathe. He could go on doing this forever. It was altogether different from being out of air. It was being free of having to breathe, like the Honors he had seen dancing around the Thorn with the bubbles from their fresh kills, dancing all night, hey, and gulping the Amsir-wind from the bubbles, but never breathing, just blowing out once in every while and mouthing the disembodied parts of Amsir chest again, laughing and whooping, like the dead were said to whoop with joy on Ariwol.

The Amsir's body was dying now. Its head might be dead, or it might live forever, but who could tell when nothing but skin connected it to the body and it had no wind to shriek with? The eyes were shut. There was something thick and clear seeping out between the closed lids and drying immediately to a crust. The wing tips were still quivering. But Honor White Jackson was a hell of a lot more alive than it was, and he stumbled quickly to the javelin, his throwing stick, and his darts, the one far away and the other near to hand with fresh gouges up the short Amsir-bone shaft. He got them clustered into his hands with his arms around the Amsir, and then he wandered out from beyond the outcropping's shadow, still cold but not caring, riotous as a tickled child, happy on pure oxygen, with his first Amsir like the world's most awkward bucket of cool water on a blazing day.

Chapter Two

I

When he had rested for a long time in the cool sand, watching nebulae and moons wheel by beautifully without his knowing what they were, he raised himself on one elbow and fondly stroked the Amsir's long thigh as it lay sprawled beside him. The hunting bird, wings folded, was only a dim, coverletted shape, but Honor White Jackson could have named every curled rim of horn, every trailing pennon, every nail, every tooth. He unfastened the trimmed and harnessed water bubble at the small of his back, unstoppered it and raised it to the corpse before sipping from it himself.

As his neck and back muscles stretched, sand cracked free of his wounds and tickled him as it slipped down his spine. He grinned at the Amsir and patted its hip. He stood up, hooked and tied his gear into place, and oriented himself to the shadow of the treacherous rocks against the stars. Now that he knew where he was, he could go where he had been. And now that he was standing up, he could no longer hear approaching Amsir feet if there were any such in his vicinity. So he must go.

Stooping, he hefted his first conquest, eased it down across his shoulders, and began a steady, fast and comfortable walk, broken with pauses for listening closely and looking around as well as he could. Amsirs did not seem to move much at night – hence the Honor tactic of slipping away from the Thorn at dusk and picking a good ambush in the morning. But Honor White Jackson was more than ever in an iconoclastic mood, and he wondered why, if Amsirs did not haunt the darkness, so many of those ambushes failed.

His grip on his slain enemy was needlessly rigid; he knew that, but he did not slacken it. He could have carried him more easily if he'd relaxed, but he did not do that, either.

Nobody had told him Amsirs could talk. Nobody had told him they carried metal spears, or any weapon but claws, beak, and wing tips. He had been told – all children of the Thorn were told, even before most of them drifted into farming and a very few tried to be Honors – that the Amsirs would get them all if the Honors did not watch out. But he had not been told how they would be got.

He would not let his Amsir go. He thought it was because he had had to learn so much to get him.

The gritty, sharp-faced grains of sand made noises like gentle screams beneath his trudging feet. The Amsir rustled and rattled. It was full of ridges and pointed places that goaded White Jackson's flesh. The wings were full of joints along the main bone. It was conventional to speak of the hand as growing out of the elbow, but in fact there was a joint between shoulder and hand. From the hand down, the remainder of the wing was supported by what would have been a monstrously long little finger in a man. The ribs that stiffened the wing were of hard cartilage growing from the joints of that finger, of the wrist, and of the true elbow. It was like a broken awning. No matter how Jackson folded the wings and tried to tuck them into each other or pin them under the Amsir's hard chest, the nail at the end of that little finger on one wing tip or the other would flop down and swing teasingly across his ankles as he walked. He put the Amsir down, and trussed it with its own lace. Now it was a rolling bundle on his back, stiff and contrary.

An edge on it found the deepest place Jackson was cut – a beak-furrow across the top of his shoulder, its edges stiff and gaping, crusted dry with sand, open down to the rubbery twist-surfaced muscle. Jackson was fascinated with the cut – it was unusual to be able to touch his own inside, to dwell on the thought that if he were not a victorious Honor he would be wincing pitifully. He understood perfectly well that all men would rather not put their flesh in peril. He knew from himself that even a small hurt could nag a man with reminders of why reluctance was wise. But he had noticed that it wasn't the size of the wound, it was his feeling for himself that made a man cry or not, and that was why he had become a Honor. Now he was a Honor who would have a white Amsir-beak scar across one broad shoulder; a Honor who put his Amsir down from time to time and stretched out on the sand beside him, ear to the grit, listening, with the stars and small moons giving him little to light his night by, and going back to the Thorn where he would live differently from before.

II

It was very nearly dawn when he caught the loom of the Thorn against the low stars. At the same time, he noticed a human step on the sand. He thought it might be Black Jackson coming towards him around the shoulder of a dune.

The way it was supposed to go, a Honor was discovered sitting beside his kill on the sun side of the Thorn when the people got up in the morning. Successful Honors had been known to stay out on the edge of the desert all night, even when they didn't have to. People who accidentally came across a Honor before dawn pretended the man didn't have a carcase across his back. The idea was to create an effect that it had all just somehow happened, like a meteorite shower. The Honor was supposed to play it very cool too, and not notice that anybody was paying any attention to him – at least until there was enough of an audience for him to suddenly break out in a big happiness.

All that guff got more comment than it did attention. It seemed to be a hangover from some time maybe half a dozen generations back when some nut had whipped up a lot of pious ritual. The trouble with any of this stuff that was supposed to make life better and more interesting was that life plain never did get any better, and a man still had to find his own interests. After a while even a community of farmers could notice that. So White had half expected, especially on his first kill, that a live head like Black Jackson would be around to give him a personal handshake, or something, before discovering him all over again in the morning. To say nothing of the fact that just maybe, even though it wasn't like a Honor was supposed to be, Black might be worried.

The Amsir was suddenly beginning to get that characteristic smell Jackson had studied from boyhood. He pulled his cap off cautiously, and sure enough he was inside the comfortable radius, even if it was still very much like desert underfoot and breathing took a little work in the chill air. It was a lot farther out than the farmers cared to come. Farther in, there would be a good four dozen feet of weedy grass around the perimeter before the fields began. Winters, that strip shrank to something that was still wider than two dozen. For a part of the year, when the days were long, and the high sun beat down sharply on the glistening gridwork atop the Thorn, the strip might be close to five. The fields never crept out into it. A farmer, White Jackson had decided early, was anybody who would scheme nights to edge an inch off his neighbour's boundary but wouldn't reach for the title to all Ariwol if he'd ever cut his finger on an edge of parchment.

It *was* Black Jackson, tall and with muscle around his stomach and waist that White Jackson envied the hell out of, his short hair marking him as a made Honor. His bare face showed up in a paler patch against the dark contrast of his mouth and eye-pits. White stopped, but didn't let the Amsir slide to the ground, and stood easily.

'Welcome, Honor,' Black said. There was something unusually breathy in his big rumble of a voice, which, for many years, White had been thinking of as strong but friendly. Black came forward and touched White on the shoulder – the sound one, as it happened. Although it was still pretty nearly full dark, at this distance White could see the sober set of Black's broad mouth. This was beginning to relax as Black touched the Amsir. White had noticed long ago that people believed only what they touched – the rest they believed conditionally, on the testimony of people who claimed to have touched. 'You all right, kid?' Black touched him again.

'Uh-huh.'

'Well. Well, you got one, didn't you? And you're okay.' Black was walking around him, displaying more and more of a species of relief, studying the Amsir, poking the carcase. 'Young one,' he said, appraising the calluses on the pads of its toes with a rasp of his thumb. He had been carrying his dart and stick. He put these down and looked at White. 'Give you a lot of trouble?'

White shrugged.

Black had found the javelin across White's shoulders under the Amsir's body. It slid easily into his hands.

'Come at you with this, did he?'

'Uh-huh.'

Black's glance came up fast from under his lowered brows. 'Say anything?'

'Nothing much.'

'What did he say?'

'Something about how he had me, I guess. I was busy. And he called me a wet devil.'

'Any more?'

'No. I killed him about then.'

Black bent to examine the Amsir's neck. He fingered the edges of the dart punch. 'Nice work. Caught him clean.'

'Well, that's how Black Jackson taught me.'

'Kid?'

'Yeah?'

'Feels good, doesn't it?' Black Jackson was grinning. Whether he knew it or not, he looked as if he was remembering, not as if he was enjoying now. And it looked as if he was working hard to remember. 'Going out there, getting your first one . . . finding out just how tough you are?'

'You mean, it felt good for you when you did it.'

'Well, yeah. Yeah, kid. I remember how – '

'How tough am I, Black?'

'I don't follow you.'

'I mean, you're the one that's making happy about what I found out. Do you know what I found out?'

'Well, sure. I . . . Look, I don't hold it against anybody they didn't tell *me* Amsirs had spears and could talk!'

White Jackson had been thinking about this ever since the first screech out of the Amsir's mouth. But he had never seen his brother this way before. He studied Black as closely as he had studied the Amsir who had taken off from the blown ambush but hadn't really tried to outrun him. 'I figured maybe we could pass a few words about it.' He was thinking about a throwing spear that had at least as much range as a Honor's dart, and a Amsir who nevertheless hadn't pulled out to a safe distance and then picked him off – and also hadn't stood and fought until he was ready.

'Point is, you didn't need to be told, did you? Got him anyhow, right?' Black had the javelin head-down in the sand beside his foot, and was leaning on it. That way, it looked like a stick of some kind and not much of a weapon. 'And I told you they were tricky. Remember?' he said as an afterthought.

'Uh-huh.' He held tighter to his Amsir. He believed this was because he had a stupid feeling Black might try to take it away. He believed he had the stupid feeling because he had suddenly realized Black wasn't going to give the spear back. He waited for Black to say something. It was Black who obviously knew what was going to happen here next.

'Well, ain't it something to go out against something that's that tough, and come back carrying it?'

'It's something.'

Black was wrapping and unwrapping his thick fingers around the javelin's shaft. The sharp metal head gritted down, sinking deeper. 'It gives you the feel of being a man, right?'

'It gives me the feeling of something. I was a man before I went out there.'

Black tipped him lightly, awkwardly with his clenched fist, this time on his bad shoulder. He couldn't see it was bad. 'You always were tough. Never gave an inch. You'd cut me down just as soon as you would one of those kids you used to bloody up. If I wasn't your brother, I mean . . . And bigger, I guess.'

This was not the view White had had of himself through his brother's eyes. And this wasn't the talk he had expected. It was teaching him a lot more about Black than it was about Amsir-honning, and he didn't want to be taught any more about his brother. He had been perfectly satisfied with what he had believed up to now.

'Black, it's getting on to first light,' White said softly. 'I have to go sit by the Thorn. Come mid-morning, the Eld Honor's got to look over my Amsir, see it's real, call me a Honor, chop my hair, name a winning man to shave me; that'd be you, I guess. Be a busy day for both of us. Why don't we just call me a made Honor for now and let me pick up any other tricks of the trade as I go along?'

A foot of the javelin's length was buried in the ground. It occurred to White that Black only had a third of a dozen feet to go before he had it out of sight entirely. 'No, look – kid, it could of been somebody else waiting here to meet you. We all get met the first time. It's – hell, you can see it's necessary. But it could have been Red Filson or Black Harrison or one of those other guys that hang around the Eld a lot. It didn't have to be me. But I trained you – same way I was trained; we all get trained the same way – when you get back, you see the good in that –'

'If you get back.'

'*You?* Hell, I knew *you'd* get back!'

'Sure.'

'Well, I figured you had a good chance.' Black twisted the javelin; White couldn't decide whether he was really trying to bury it right here or whether he was so wrapped up in his words that he wasn't even thinking about his hands. A trait like that could get a Honor killed. White had to assume it was rare. '*Good* chance,' Black said stubbornly.

'All right,' White said, feeling the cracks in his lips where the edges of the Amsir's chest wound had cut them.

'Listen, kid, there's a lot more to growing up besides getting your hair chopped!' White noticed that Black was getting angry in the same way as when somebody refused to believe it about the caps. 'You think we're gonna let a bunch of punk kids – even Honor kids – run around tellin' the farmers all about what it takes to be a Honor? You think those farmers don't all believe *they* could be Honors if they could spare the time? You think it don't make a difference to a Honor, taking a piece of a farmer's loaf, to *know* he couldn't be?'

'Because he's a Honor who got back from his first time.'

'That's right. Now you're getting it. It ain't what you're taught – it's what you *are* that makes a Honor!' Black looked proudly across at his brother, at a man whom he could consider a man like himself. He jerked the spear out of the ground and brandished it. 'Because you went up against *this.*'

That, and talk from animals, and caps that didn't work, and brothers who spent years getting you ready for the night they lurked to check you out on the way back in. White Jackson looked at this powerful simpleton who had raised him. He didn't know whether he was supposed to swallow this line because he was dumb enough to believe it or because Black was dumb enough to believe it. Either way, Black was not the man White had thought him, and in that case what brains did White have to brag about?

'All right. I've got it.'

Black looked at him sidelong in the growing greyness. 'You sure, kid?' He was begging for the right answers. He was being very gruff and tough about it, but he was begging. White guessed that in his own simple way Black loved him and was sweating out the payoff for the years in which he had prepared the greatest gift he knew to give. 'I mean you're not going to say anything different, are you? I want you to be sure in your own mind you're not going to pop off to the people until you've had a chance to talk to the Eld Honor about it. Lots of times, the Eld Honor can explain it all in a minute or two. Explain it a hell of a lot better than *I* can, that's for sure,' he realized.

White shook his head. 'I'm going to play it the way every new Honor plays it. I'm going to tell a story about ambushing him and having a hell of a fight and winning out in the end, and that's all.'

'You sure?'

'You're damned right I'm sure.'

Black began to sigh with relief, but White was mad at him now, and wasn't going to let him off the hook.

'Now you tell the Eld Honor something for me. You tell him I want to know about a metal spear even a Amsir can throw farther than I can flip a dart. Hell, a human could throw it eight dozen yards into an eye, and just how many of 'em do we have cached away? I want to know why my hat didn't work when I was behind a rock. I want to know about Amsirs that talk. You tell him for me I think he's got rotten brains for letting a brother come out to talk to me. You're so shook up I *could* take you – even if I wasn't expecting you to try for me.' He finished slowly: 'You got that last part all sorted out, Black? I do. I got it sorted out fine about a Honor out here with weapons but no hat. There's only a couple of things a Honor could kill out here with that rig. One of them's poor slob Honors tryin' to crawl back with spearholes in 'em that couldn't be explained, and the other one's young Honors that won't shut up about what kind of people we're sharin' Creation with. On the short end of the share. Now you just go take that spear and put it wherever all the other spears are; I'm not gonna go around upsetting the Honor racket, especially now I made my way into it, but don't you mess me around until I'm over this.'

He swung away and his Amsir rattled on his shoulders smelling like hell. He realized he was simple for giving Black so many excuses to just give that spear a little toss in the name of whatever Black thought was decent. But whenever White got mad and didn't show it, he was always crying sick inside for days. He figured if he just kept walking away from his brother who loved him, he had an even chance of getting off.

Chapter Three

I

It was warm and pleasant in the sun. He sat cross-legged with his back against the warm black-and-brown flank of the Thorn. His eyes were slitted into the sunrise, and he was only a little bit conscious of the people filtering out of the low cement dwellings that ringed the Thorn, beyond the running track.

The running track made a clear space of bare dirt a couple of dozen yards around the Thorn, and was a dozen times a dozen dozen yards long from start to start. Red Filson, long-legged and looking like he knew everything about anything – from the scar that lifted his mouth and the corner of his left eye – was running a group of young Honor-types around it. As they went by White Jackson, the sound of bare feet thudding first in his right ear and then in his left, the young ones rolled their eyes sidewards at the spread-winged Amsir sprawled beside him.

Filson, sun-bleached lank blond hair all spiky with sweat, just grinned his grinless grin and kept eating up ground with his feet, with that smooth, scissoring motion that had run down a lot of things. One of the things had been Black Olson, who had been Black and White Jackson's father. Still was their father, White supposed, but was dead, run down with his throwing arm stabbed through and his eyes blinded from a cut across the brows.

Truth to tell, White hadn't seen an awful lot of the old man after his naming day. It seemed like he'd no sooner found out Dad's first name was Jack than he was part of a Honor candidate class like this class of Filson's. White was supposed to be mojoed by the worry that between a running father and a farmer mother no Jackson could stand up with Red Filson. White wasn't ready to swear what went on in Black Jackson's mind, with all its side steps, but as for White, he had noticed long ago he wasn't either his mother or his father. He sat smiling faintly into the sun, his arms dangling over his thighs. The class went on by in its circuit, the young ones sweating and grunting, Red sweating and grinning. White was thinking that being strung out mad about being mojoed would be a handy excuse if he ever decided there was something he didn't want to share with Honor Red Filson.

The sun did feel good. Now that he was sitting down and didn't have to do anything but wait for other people to do things, White could let himself feel sleepy. And he was where he had spent a lot of time wanting to be. Up against the Thorn, feeling its pitted warm surface comfortably rough against his back, and the sweetish scent of the Amsir rising around him. He could turn loose of things he had held tight for a long time. He gazed through his lashes at the half-focused sight of the green fields and orchards beyond the houses, with the shadows of gathering people moving across the corners of his eyes.

Listening to them talk to each other – like a cross between things crackling far away and a mumble like the sound of whatever went on inside the Thorn – a man felt as good as a baby in his crib. His back was safe, and nobody in front could do anything to him right now. A lot of them would never dare to do anything anytime from now on, just because he had killed something and would be short-haired. The rest of them would think long and hard about messing around a Honor's goods or women. The idea was, Honors looked out for each other. It worked out they did look out for each other, when it was between Honor and farmer, so from now on there wouldn't be a farmer or even a Honor-type who would buck him to his face. And damned few who would go for his back, even when they had a good chance.

He had really messed up that Amsir, too. Given him one hell of a shock, with all the plans of that horned brain notching into each other, and the wet devil lying there helpless, and all of a sud –

What was it like to die? White wondered. Get cut off like that, in the middle of being alive, in the middle of thinking you had it made. Did you have time to know you were a chump? And just suppose there was an Ariwol. Suppose you were a human and a Amsir had done that to you, and you turned up among the happy dead with all of that chumpiness slopping around inside you. Yeah, sure, everybody laughing and singing, feast going on all the time, but man, the ones who hadn't died chumpy would have an extra laugh on you, and all the chumps would try to buddy up. But that was a tricky idea to live up to, because sure as there was sand in Creation that Amsir hadn't thought he was being a chump, he had thought he was on top right up to *punch*!

Well, how could the Amsir know White Jackson had watched the Honors around the Thorn with their fresh bubbles? How could he know White Jackson would remember that, would trust that, wouldn't try to breathe what couldn't be breathed, would wait for what his enemy had to give him? Was it being a chump to be happy when your plan worked out? It was, White Jackson decided, when you didn't know all about what it was having to work against. And how do you know all about what's inside a head?

There were more people gathering around him. Just standing there, with their farmer tools in their hands, the women with their water buckets, their kids . . . farmers not going out, women not lining up at the taps in the side of the Thorn, kids playing Honor behind the crowd, hanging on to grownup legs up front.

What do they know? White Jackson thought to himself, watching the sun, smelling his Amsir, letting himself notice his shoulder and his other cuts just enough to remind himself. All they see is me and a dead one. No – all they see is the outsides of the two of us. What do they know about that we found out? And if they had been there and watched us do it, would they know any more? Touch me – any one of you, touch me or touch him, and you'll find out the last thing there is. How's about it, you muckers – anybody want to ride to Ariwol on the end of a dart this morning?

Filson and his candidates came around the Thorn again, Filson in front now, not running sweat but with a nice allover bead worked up, the candidates pale as lace and soaking wet, their eyes blind. They were one less – somebody had turned farmer after all, lying sucking wind somewhere around the curve of the Thorn with dirt in his mouth and water in his eyes. White Jackson thought about that scar on Filson there; Red had come back from his first hon with that on him. Filson knew. White wanted to grin at him as he went by. But he wouldn't have known if he was really getting an answer. He'd have to figure out what was inside that head. And, hell, Black Olson hadn't been able to figure that, had he? Welcome to Ariwol, Olson.

Petra Jovans came walking up to the edge of the crowd, making a little space around herself, as usual, and stood there with her hands folded in front of her abdomen, just looking at him with all of that quiet in her eyes. What do you know? White Jackson thought, testing it on her, and then he wished he knew the things she knew; how to look at somebody for sure. Keep your hands off, but eyes are all right. Yes, I'm going to be damned good for you when you're what I expect.

He wondered whether it would really be with her that he first exercised some of his new rights as Honor Secon Black Jackson. Well, anyway, with somebody. Then sooner or later a son would be old enough to name, and people would learn his own name was Jim. Then someday he'd leave off honning and be Honor Grey Jackson, and maybe there'd be a Honor Jimson or a farmer named Jim Petras to scatter his bones and maybe not. Somebody'd scatter 'em, that was sure, because whether they did it out of grief or anything else they felt, the idea was to make damn sure that the old man was dead. Sitting there, looking at it that way, White Jackson could see that if he was lucky enough to have all of this happen without ugly interruptions out in the desert, it was still a short damn list of important things left to have happen in his life.

It came to him he'd spent a lot of years running around the Thorn and pitching darts to come to the moment he realized it was all downhill from here on. But it *was* all downhill, and when he thought of all the people he'd seen follow that road, and the way they did it because they'd all heard the elders telling them and telling them how to do it, White Jackson realized that the track to Ariwol was beaten many times as hard as the track around the Thorn.

What do you know? he thought to all the people. I could die sitting here, all punched out inside like Red Thompson was that time last year. The first anybody knew was when the Eld Honor touched him and he fell over just as stiff as his Amsir. I could be doing that, and when you found out you'd say Oh hell, what a shame. But when I get up in a minute you'll make all kinds of noises except that. And just the same I'm dying. I wish there was a puddle of blood under *me.* You'd say the right thing then. What *do* you know?

Petra had drifted into the crowd in such a way that she was right in his line of vision. Because he was thinking that she knew, if anybody knew, that he was as dead this minute as the farmers had been from birth, he winked at her. He realized he was getting a little crazy, but it seemed reasonable to get that way when you were dying and you'd been fighting animals that were people inside and had a fine brother like Black who was too simple to either beg your pardon or kill you and get it over.

White Jackson was wondering where the failed Honors' graveyard was, out there beyond the fields, when the Eld Honor came through the crowd and touched him on the shoulder.

'Arise, Honor – you are home with your kill!' the old man said in a loud voice. He was all knobs and bones under his brown shrunken skin. His cheeks were in deep where his teeth had been, and his eyes were pouched. If he had had wings, he would have been fair game. 'You all right, son?' he asked in a low voice.

White could see Black hanging off around the edge of the crowd with a lot of other Honors. 'Black talk to you?' he said to the old man without moving his lips. It wasn't all that unusual to see Honors carrying their weapons around the Thorn, but there were quite a few of them doing that. White would have been happier if on this particular day he didn't see so much sun on so many dartheads.

'Yes.' For the crowd the Eld Honor said, 'The people are waiting to praise you.' His hand on White's shoulder had a lot of knuckles in it. His voice changed again. 'What do you think of them?'

White looked frankly and fully into the old man's eyes. 'As near to what you think as makes no difference.'

'Hmm. Was Black right in passing you?' the Eld Honor asked, which surprised the daylights out of White. But the rheumy old eyes were tight on his. Maybe the old man expected he could tell a liar that way. Maybe he could.

'As far as you and me go, he was right.' That might not have been quite what Eld Honor had been expecting, either, but it was what White had for him. It was more than what White intended to give him. Some of that stuff they told kids might really work – always give the Eld a straight answer, never do anybody dirt, that kind of thing. Parts of it seemed to stick better than others.

They were blowing time. The Eld Honor's mouth was working at the corners, and he was looking at White the way a farmer looked at his new wife's first loaf. But they couldn't keep testing each other out here forever. The pressure on the Eld was a lot worse than it was on White, as far as White could see. Seeing it suddenly as he did, he relaxed inside as happily as ever a man did when he unstopped a bubble on a hot day and felt the cool water going all the way in to the pit of his stomach. He was ready to go on this way forever. The old man had to move, he didn't; the old man was the one who would have to think up the story if he had White killed now. And White was saying things that didn't really give an excuse. They were just aggravating.

'So you think we're equals,' the Eld said. 'You think you've lived one day longer and all of a sudden even your brother and his friends are dumb, and only the Eld is fit for a man like you to be frank with. Must be a happy day when a young man picks his peer from the decrepit.' It was hard to tell when a mouth like that was smiling faintly. 'Well, all right – you'll get your badges and tokens, and we'll talk afterwards.' The old man raised his voice. 'See here!' he cried. 'A man sits with his kill!'

That, of course, was the signal for a lot of general roaring and shouting and people pushing forward. There were things to do, and the Eld Honor pointed out people to do them –

Black Jackson would do the shaving – and White Jackson found that becoming a made Honor meant you had to shake hands with people like Filson, and get punched around by a bunch of farmers who considered that touching you was the price of admission for standing around and staring at a dead Amsir, which was what they all went off and did as soon as they were through assuring themselves that White Jackson was real. 'Keep it short,' the Eld Honor said, as he led White Jackson forward to where the shaving bowl was waiting.

'Uh-huh,' White Jackson said, looking back over his shoulder. Black Harrison and Red Filson were guarding his Amsir. You still couldn't tell whether Filson was grinning, but you could tell about Harrison, and he was.

So his hair was chopped short and he was shaved by his brother's steady hand, and they called him Honor Secon Jackson to the crowd, and the crowd grinned and laughed. Secon Jackson stood there with his head chilly and thought: Oh, you people, you dumb, happy people! You're killing me.

Chapter Four

I

'Well, ah, Secon, you certainly brought back one with flesh on him,' said Mowery Sals, who was a grainy-necked farmer already. There was a time when Boy Jackson and Boy Samson, who was Mowery now, had been playmates. That was just about the same time Dorrie Olsons had been widowed and gone to be Dorrie Filsons. Boy Samson had remarked on it to Jackson, and that had lost him his name right there; you don't keep up with the other apprentice Honors when your ribs are fresh broken.

But here he was now, with his eyes big and his face sweating for the chance to touch a Honor, and there seemed to be no malice in him at all.

The idea was, there'd be a feast around the Thorn this evening, an Amsir-butchering, and Secon Jackson was now supposed to pick the people who'd eat his bird and get what parts. He was supposed to pick out people who'd been especially nice or good to him in his younger life. Leaving the feast to wait between noon and dark gave people he'd left out a chance to curry favour. He didn't know whether that last part was on purpose or not, but he'd seen a lot of Honors turn up a lot of bright new friends and riches on the afternoon of Shaving Day.

Well, Secon's father was a long time dead, and his mother had done what she did with Red Filson, and his brother had done his best to raise him, when he had time, but then there was that business this morning. He didn't have any kindly uncle or aunts, not being a farmer bred, and he didn't have any friends.

He might have had some friends this morning, but they were all going to have to go out into that desert pretty soon themselves, and he didn't want them around to listen to a pack of lies this evening. So here everybody was, looking at him expectantly, and the Eld Honor shuffling off from the edge of the crowd to go inside the Thorn where the Honors lived, and Secon didn't have a thing to say.

'Look,' he said, looking around at them, thinking he could try saying Petra Jovans's name and see how they liked having him pick her out in front of everybody. 'I got to go do something about this,' he said, pointing to the wound on his shoulder. 'I'll be seein' my friends during this day.' He pushed his way past Mowery, and his brother, and a disappointed sound from the people. He heard some talk about how he was auctioning off the Amsir to the highest bidders, and he didn't give a damn about that because he was expecting it. His brother pushed up next to him and walked beside him.

'Hey, that ain't no way to do!' Black Jackson said.

'If I did what I oughta do, you'd have holes in you,' Secon Jackson said and kept walking.

He went into the Thorn through the oval doorway as if he'd been doing it all his life. They taught you that; you memorized the whole layout, drawing it in the dirt with a stick, so you'd know where the Eld Honor was, and you'd know where the armoury was, and the doctor, and where you would sleep when you came back from the desert after killing your animal.

It was so the farmers would think a species of great enlightenment had fallen on you, and the kids tagging along could crane their necks and see how sure you were. They stopped short at the door, of course, because they knew anybody that wasn't a Honor would sicken and die right away if he stepped across the high threshold. White Jackson had got through the door and peeked up a couple or three inside corridors while he was a kid. He hadn't sickened and died. But he'd been smart enough not to do it on a dare, or when anybody was watching, and he'd had the idea well in mind that if he was caught he might wish he could sicken and die. Besides, all he'd learned was that the inside of the Thorn was just as much metal as the outside, except it was painted.

There was a lot of thumping and humming inside the Thorn; the metal floor shook under his feet. There were great big parts to the Thorn's inside layout that he hadn't been taught. He figured that was because those were places where the machinery was. Something had to be giving power to the ploughs. Something had to be making the water that came out of the taps, and that ran out into the fields to make the crops grow. He didn't believe that the dead in Ariwol would bother to take time out from the feasting to do all that by magic. If they could, what was there a Thorn for in the first place?

Now he had to figure the Thorn ran the hats too, and, that being the way it was, he was less ready than ever to believe in magic from something that could be stopped by a hunk of rock. Maybe they'd let him get a look at some of those mechanical insides, if he was a good boy and played along. He wondered if he could ever work things around to where they'd let him fool with it, though, and what was the good of machinery you couldn't fool with? So what was the good of playing along? And besides, Petra Jovans hadn't tried to talk to him at all while he was on his way from the shaving bowl to the door to the Thorn, and so he was pretty mad about everything as he found the Eld Honor's door and stepped inside.

'You don't knock?' the Eld Honor said from behind the table where he was sitting.

'You weren't expecting me?' Honor Secon Jackson said.

The Eld Honor grinned – there wasn't any doubt about it this time; he grinned as big as Secon Jackson had ever seen on anyone, and in some way that scared him.

'Sit down, Honor,' the Eld said, pushing a chair out to him. 'I think there's a way we can get along pretty well.'

The chair was exactly the kind of thing that everybody had in his house, except this one hadn't been used for so many years by so many people. Its wheels still rolled. Secon Jackson took it, nudged it around to where the desk was clearly between him and the Eld Honor, and sat down. 'All right. I wouldn't mind.'

'I wouldn't mind, either, if I were you,' the Eld Honor said. 'Let's not mistake the situation, Honor Secon Jackson. I've been alive a long time, and there was a day for me too when I went out in the desert and got my little surprise.

Every Honor you see walking around this place – every Honor who's ever told you anything about honning and Amirs – has gone out and had the same surprise. You don't hear any of them complaining. And you don't see me having any trouble running things. Think about that. Don't do anything that looks good to you. Whatever it is I've already thought of it.'

Secon Jackson studied him the same way he always studied things. The grin was a lot less, now, but it was still there. Secon Jackson tried to think what he'd be thinking if he had that grin; that didn't often do much good, but this time it worked. It had the feel of truth all over it. The old man was thinking what a fool Secon Jackson would make of himself, and how easy he'd be to handle, if he went ahead and did what looked like a perfectly sensible thing to him. All right, Secon Jackson thought, then I won't do it, and the next move is yours.

'So you're not going to get anything special out of me just for having done what every other live Honor in this place has done.'

I knew that a minute ago, Secon Jackson said to himself, and then he realized that the old man could have that grin and still be making a fool of himself. He knew Secon Jackson was fast, but he didn't believe how fast. There's more Amsir to you than just your looks, old man, Secon Jackson thought, feeling better, and how would you like to go up to Ariwol right now and find out about being chumpy?

'Don't plan to kill me now,' the Eld said carelessly. 'I'll die soon enough, and then you can have it all.'

II

It was like having extra distance put between him and his eyes and ears. Secon Jackson leaned back in his chair and said, 'I can.'

'Yes, you can. But I have to tell you how, and you have to learn how, and you have to learn how to make it stick.'

'All right,' said Secon Jackson, coming back to himself, 'start in on your part of that.'

The Eld Honor looked amused. 'Well, I can't give it all to you in one day.'

'I didn't expect you could, but start in.'

'All right. Look – things are very simple here. We tell the people a lot of garbage to make it look tricky, but it's simple. We live around the Thorn, here, and out beyond the Thorn is a desert with Amsirs on it. We can grow crops, and we can get some meat and some tool-stuff from honning the Amsirs. Now that's all there is to the world. The sun comes up, the sun goes down. There's summer, there's winter. There's just so much land, and there are just so many hats to give to the Honors. Now, that's all got to be managed. If we let the farmers alone, they'd do whatever was easiest, and they'd sit around having babies and planting whatever came into their heads, and there might be enough food or there might not. And even if there was enough food – which I don't think the farmers could see to – everybody'd live exactly the same. Would you like that, Honor?' The old eyes were twinkling.

'You don't need an answer for that. Go on.'

'All right, I don't need an answer. Now all you can see is the top of the system. You see the way we've been kidding the farmers, and you see the things we do to make the farmers think we're something special. That way, when we need something to keep this place running, we can have it. When we see a woman we want we can have her. Now let's talk about women. What's a woman for – besides making jokes?'

'Cooking, cleaning, keeping house,' Secon Jackson said.

The Eld Honor was shaking his head, which didn't surprise Jackson because you don't ask questions if you don't already know a tricky answer. 'No,' the Eld Honor said wisely, 'a woman is for being better than your mother, so you can have sons who are better than you. Remember that. It's the same way about everything else. When you take a farmer's loaf of bread, and you eat that bread, the reason for that bread is to make you better – to keep you strong, and to make you a better Honor. And if one farmer's woman's bread is better than another's, then you go back to that place for your bread. Even if you never take that woman – and she might be old and ugly. But she might have a daughter, and you can take that daughter. And even if she doesn't have a daughter, you're still better and stronger, from the better bread, and you can take a better woman than you could have otherwise. And even if you don't take her, but you just use her, and her kid turns out to be a farmer, he's going to be a better farmer than he would have been, 'cause we already know his mother's man wasn't good enough to stop you.'

'So we're always making it better, no matter what we do,' Secon Jackson said. It occurred to him that it was a pretty nice world where a Honor could do any damn thing that struck his fancy, and it always made things better. 'Now explain about Amsirs that carry spears and talk.'

'We'll get to that, I promise you,' the Eld Honor said. 'The reason we don't ever take a chance of anybody's finding out until he becomes a Black Honor is the same reason we don't spell any of this out where the farmers can hear it.' The Eld Honor leaned forward earnestly. 'Now this is important, boy. If you can understand and use this, there will be a reason for you to be somebody special, even among Honors.'

The Eld gestured negligently. 'Hell, I know most of the boys who carry weapons around here are just farmers with a different kind of plough. Instead of knowing how to thresh wheat, they know how to jump Amsirs, and as long as they know that, they figure it makes them special enough, and that's all the thinking they'll ever have to do. No, boy – ' The Eld pointed a dried old skinny finger at him. '*You* have to be like *us* – you have to have eyes in your head, and ears, and something in between them. You know that much as well as I do. What I know a lot better than you is how.

'There's a whole bunch of people around here and every one of them thinks he's someday going to go to Ariwol the same as everybody else, and live high without working. You let him hold on to that, because it makes him work while he's here, all right. You let him be a farmer, or a Honor, but you let him keep thinking about Ariwol, where *his* kind of people are on top for sure. But you make sure he knows he's a farmer, or a Honor, because then he knows who he is, and he knows what's expected of him while he's here.

'If he knows what's expected of him, then he'll do what's expected. He won't start snooping around in the middle of the night, or in a bunch in the middle of the day, and pull the props right out from under everything that's being done for him. How many of *us* do you think there are in any generation? It's a damn small number, boy. What all of the farmers and most of the Honors aren't ever going to admit to themselves is, if it wasn't for us they'd all be dead. They'd be dead from ruining the land, or they'd be dead from eating wrong, or they'd be dead because they'd be messing around inside here, and they'd kill the Thorn.'

The Eld studied Secon Jackson's face. 'Now have you ever heard of anybody wanting to get into the Thorn that wasn't entitled to? But do you see any guards around? Have you ever heard of a farmer suddenly saying "I'm gonna go out and hon Amsirs"? Have you ever heard of a farmer saying "I want more water"? And let me ask you: if we had guards out front, wouldn't the farmers say "I wonder what they're guarding. And if it needs guards, maybe all I have to do to understand it is knock somebody out of my way"? No, boy, you ever thought what would happen if we said to the farmers: "You can't go Amsir-honning." Wouldn't they stop to wonder "Well, hell, that's just a rule they're making up"? No, boy, you don't do that, or you have the whole mess of it milling around and figuring that all it has to do is break a few rules and it can have whatever it wants. You show it an open doorway, and you say to it "That's for Honors," You send people out into the desert, and a lot of them don't come back. You don't have to tell the farmers that's just for Honors – not doing it that way, you don't. They can see for themselves.

'That's the way you run things, boy. And I'll tell you something else – I'll bet you there are farmers who have gone out into the desert, and I'll bet you there are people who have come through that front doorway. But they didn't tell anybody they were going to do it. And they either got all the way out into the desert, and died, or they came back from the edge of the desert, and they hadn't seen a Amsir, and they didn't tell anybody about it. I don't think any of them got very far. Not because they died, but because they knew from everything around them since they were kids that they should be ashamed. And even if they saw a Amsir, or even if somebody came in here and saw things, he wouldn't know what they meant because nobody ever told him. And after a while he'd just go away again. And if he didn't sicken and die, he wouldn't tell anybody about that, either, because anybody he told just might kill him to correct the oversight. Nobody loves a loner, boy – 'cause nobody knows who he is.'

Secon Jackson looked back into the old man's tightly squeezed eyes. 'Unless he's on top.'

The old man smiled and nodded. 'That's the idea.'

'All right,' Jackson said. 'Now, besides the fact that you want some of your young Honors to get killed, how come I didn't get told that Amsirs could talk and had spears?'

'Well, you would have started making yourself a shield and a long spear before you went out there,' the Eld Honor said. 'And if we had told somebody like your brother before *he* went out, he just would have had to tell somebody, to show he knew something nobody else did. Either way, it would have got the farmers pretty well worked up. Listen, boy – what did the Amsir say to you?'

'He said "Yield".'

The Eld was already nodding – it was another one of those questions he knew the answer to. 'Exactly. He didn't want to kill you – you'd have to be a lucky damn fool not to have known that almost from the start and still be alive, and you're not a damn fool. I'm not sure you're lucky, either. Boy, there is more to the world than anybody knows – '

'I know that. Figured it out all by myself,' said Honor Secon Black Jackson, who was tired of being called 'boy'.

'Did you? And did you figure out what it means? Have you had time since it happened to do the same thinking that the farmers would do if they knew about it, and had time enough to mull it over? Listen, boy, in this world – in this *real* world that's got to be a lot bigger than just the Thorn and the desert – there's something that doesn't want to kill Honors. There's something that wants to take them away, instead. He wanted you to be his prisoner. He and every other Amsir that has let himself be ambushed out there was willing to take the chance of dying because he was playing out some plan, while all the Honor wanted to do was kill him.

'Something out there wants Honors. Maybe it just wants to eat them alive, in comfort someplace, out of the desert. I don't know – nobody does. But whatever it is, the way it looks is there's a world big enough so that Honors aren't even farmers to it – they're a crop. And how long do you think we could run this place around here if the farmers knew that was what we were?'

Secon Jackson sat there waiting for more, but the Eld was sitting back in his chair, and looking at him as if he'd expected him to be knocked over. For a minute there, Jackson couldn't believe it. The Eld had told him all this, just to make a point that Jackson had figured out for himself last night in the long walk home. All this aggravation, all this listening to an old man talk, when he could have been doing something useful, and here was the big pack the old man had unwrapped for him, and there was nothing in it – nothing – that wasn't second-hand.

You old man, he thought, you've been wasting our time. He said: 'So you figure I'm smart enough. If I learn how to keep in line without shovin', one of these days I'll get to be the Eld Honor?'

'You could. You've got the best chance of anybody.' The old man looked at him steadily, with his lie-detecting stare. 'But you're going to have to earn it. It's a hard world, boy, you can see it's harder than you ever figured. Nothing comes easy, not even for one of us.'

'One of us smart ones,' Honor Secon Jackson said.

'One of us smart ones,' the old man agreed. 'No sense kidding yourself about that – you look at yourself any other way, and you're licked before you start.'

'You seen many smart ones in your time?'

'Some.'

'Some walking around out there now, figuring they're gonna be the Eld. Each one of them, off by himself inside his own head, figuring it that way?'

The old man smiled. 'Some. Worry you?'

Jackson shook his head. 'No.'

Now the old man grinned again. It was almost as if he were getting ready to yell 'Yield! Yield!' He said: 'Got to be that way, boy. Got to have it out – got to fight. That's what makes things better; the hammering and the stabbing. It's what gives everything its shape; it's what gouges out the weak places. Boy, this place has *got* to be made better. It has got to stand up to some day when the Amsirs figure a way to get closer to the Thorn. It has got to be that way so we toughen up enough to live here if the Thorn ever goes.' The old man stood up sharply and lightly kicked the metal wall behind him. The flat of his bony old palm spatted against it. 'This is just another damn *tool*, boy! It's got to wear out someday. Everything willing, it will be the people like *us* who have made the people in this place hard enough to do without it!' The Eld's eyes were shining. He was shaking. 'Boy you've got to see!'

'See ahead. See what's gonna happen,' Jackson said.

'That's right! That's what makes *us*!'

I see, Honor Secon Black Jackson thought. I see what's ahead. I could be like you. 'Funny,' he said.

'I knew you weren't like the others before you ever went out there. Don't you think I would have been disappointed and mad if you hadn't come back? And I *have* given you something special – I've given you knowledge.'

'Yeah, well, that what I had in mind,' Jackson said. He stood up, reaching across his chest to touch his shoulder again. 'I better go see about this. Bad time to heal up crippled, now.'

III

He went down to the doctor's room. The doctor was a Grey Honor who'd got a long, twisty slash across his stomach a long time ago. He walked a little bent over all the time, and his mouth was always tight. But as long as he could doctor, the Eld would see he got food and anything else a full Honor was entitled to. When Jackson walked in, he grunted and looked at him with deep eyes: 'Your first, eh?'

'Got off cheap. Considering.'

'Any way you can get off at all, Honor. Any way. Nothing hurts more than not being able to hurt any longer.'

'You think so?' It looked like the idea was, the doctor had a little set line he gave you; buck you up a little, buck him up a little. Well, a Honor who didn't hon needed bucking up.

'Always here to patch you up the best we can, Honor,' the doctor said, then swabbed out the gash with a clean rag dipped in boiling water and held in a pair of bone tongs.

' 'Preciate it, Doc,' Jackson said, and left after the doctor had taken a couple of stitches.

He stopped off outside the Thorn, where Harrison and Filson were still guarding his Amsir, like they were supposed to. The way of it was, when a Honor brought in his bird, the Eld picked the hardest men of the Thorn to stand guard over it. The way people changed their ideas of who was the hardest man, was when a Honor decided he could tell somebody like Harrison or Filson he would guard his own bird.

Jackson looked at one, then he looked at the other. Filson grinned at him. Or maybe he didn't. 'Your mother'll be proud of you today.' The thing was, you couldn't tell from his face how he meant it.

'I guess,' Jackson said. 'You two Honors be at my feast tonight, huh?' He nodded down at the Amsir. 'Can have any part of him you want,' he said, ''cept I don't suppose you better want the same part, huh?' He walked away, and they being guards appointed by the Eld couldn't come after him if they wanted to. He didn't stop to look back at his Amsir either. It was starting to smell pretty good, which some people considered a delicacy, but he figured this particular one had given him all it could. A lot more than it had been ready to, and he figured the credit was his, not the Amsir's.

There were all kinds of people walking around, farmer women going about their chores, and kids, and the usual sort of traffic. To anybody who looked at him, and looked like he might want to talk, Jackson just said, 'You wanna come to my feast? Come ahead.' And kept walking towards the cement hut that he had been living in most of his life alone.

Inside, it was just one room, with a pad in the corner. There were bone pegs in the walls with pieces of kit hanging on them – some of it was just kid stuff; stuff he'd made when he was just learning how to make his own tools. Play stuff. Some of it was pretty useful, but he'd gone out with his best gear, and that was still either on him or in his hand. He sat down cross-legged in the corner where he usually worked, with the featureless light coming in through the parchment window he'd stretched across the frame, where maybe there'd been some other kind of lookout when the hut was first created, and somebody'd scoffed it, or maybe when the world was made whoever made it forgot to make a window.

He reset his dartheads with fresh Amsir-hide glue from the little pot he kept bubbling in a corner. He looked around. He walked over to the big blank wall opposite the window. The cement was all sooted and streaked up where he'd practised pictures and rubbed them out and practised them again, until he was pretty well satisfied.

There were things there that he'd made, oh, half, three-quarters of a dozen years ago. The wall was pretty well taken up with this kind of thing. There were pictures of kids running, and yelling, and jumping up and down. There were pictures of farmers walking along behind their ploughs with the desert on beyond them. There was something that looked a lot like a black blur of soot, and was supposed to be the Thorn up against the stars at night, and didn't look it. He'd tried leaving blank spots on the cement to make stars, but he couldn't make stars that way. He hadn't rubbed it out, because it would have just made it even more of a blur.

There was a picture of his brother. Black would come around and look at it every once in a while, and shake his head, and say 'Is that me?' Well, no, but it was a picture of him; it was a picture of him all tensed up but smooth, with all his weight on one leg and the rest of his body flying forward with an arm out, and a throwing stick way out in front of him, and you could see the way his fingers were shaped to hold on to the end, and the way the muscles of that arm had just finished snapping out the dart and were changing to keep the fingers locked on the stick. You could see the look on his face, that White Jackson had had so much trouble getting right, and off – way off – in the distance you could see something grabbing itself that was as close to a Amsir as you could draw if the only ones you had ever seen were dead and you had never seen one running.

Secon Jackson looked around the room. There wasn't a thing here that he needed to take with him. You didn't expect a Honor to take anything out of his old place on Shaving Day; living in the Thorn, you had the Thorn armoury and you didn't have to have some kid come in and keep your room fire going. All you needed was what you could carry in your hand. People came in after a Honor moved out, if he'd been living alone, and they took away what they needed. Let's see you take that wall away, Jackson thought, but he didn't really give a damn whether they could or not.

He went over to where he'd made a shelf near the toolmaking fire, and looked at the burnt sticks he kept there, and the little pots of coloured mud. He picked up one of the sticks, and he walked around with it in his hand for a while. It felt like something was going to come of it, and he looked over at the window that was clean with light through the translucent scraped hide.

He went over and looked at it with his fingertips and the flat of his palm rubbing over it. He leaned enough of his weight against it so he was just short of breaking through, and then he brought up his right hand with the stick held as if it were a handle to something, and watched the line of black grow on the parchment.

He moved the line by moving his body. When the line had gone from its beginning to where it was done, he put in another one, and when he had enough of those he began stroking at the parchment with the worn-down angled edge of the stick, jabbing his body forward from the waist and shifting his feet until it felt as if he were walking, as if he were walking in half-light over ground so rough that his feet had to be put down carefully. But each step was almost exactly the same as the last, as if with this walk he could go a long way and was measuring out his strength against how long it would take him to get there. He saw the Thorn from far away, way out over the dunes with sunset turning the sky, and he saw the rocks nearby with their sides towards him black and grey, and with just an edge bright where he could see the last sunlight hitting the parts that faced towards the Thorn.

Down in the sand he did a man with his hat off, just landing, with his gear coming loose, and his shoulder just rolling under. Now he saw from beyond the Amsir, who had only the tip of one toe in the sand, and one wing up, and was turning with his lace beginning to stream out ahead of him, and his weight transferring towards the leg he was kicking around. The Amsir had his neck stretched forward, and his mouth open, and he was going to do something wild and wonderful in a minute.

Now all that was left to do was the fingers of the one hand you could see from this side of the Amsir. And the thing was, Honor Jackson thought as he looked at it, that the Amsir was going to miss. That leg was going to swing around just wrong. When it hit the sand the other foot would have to slide forward – not much, but enough, so that when the Amsir went to spring back towards the man, off that leg he was positioning, he would be awkward, and maybe one step later he might even stumble. If he had that hand empty of anything to give it weight. So Jackson had to draw in the spear.

Chapter Five

I

Fine, fine, he thought, looking at it for his death warrant. Now you've really done it. He picked up one of his darts and used the tip of it to cut the drawing out of its frame as quickly as he could. He slashed fast enough to be reckless, but he noticed while he was doing it that he made straight cuts, and he didn't mess up any of the drawing.

It was funny how different the room looked when he could see out. He put the dart away in his armpit, and stood there with the parchment rolled up in his hands, holding it as if it might twist away from him and go straight into the fire. But then, he thought, what's the use? One of these days, they'll gut you whether you give them an excuse or not. You wanna gut something, just the thought of wanting it makes you feel so strong you don't need excuses.

He wished he had somebody here to kill. But he couldn't kill them all and live here by himself.

He went outside, carrying his two darts and his stick, with his cap riding loose on the back of his head, and the half-full bubble of water jogging behind his back. Carrying the drawing made it awkward, because he was used to having one hand free. His shoulder hurt like blazes, and he could have used some sleep, and some food. The skin around the back of his neck, and on his ears, was itching with sunburn.

He scowled at Petra Jovans as she came stepping up to him from where she'd been waiting. All of a sudden he figured maybe he better find out for sure just how much of her was farmer. 'You want to come to my feast, too?' he said with a lot of kill in his voice.

She looked up at him with her head at an angle. 'No, I don't want to be like everybody else.' Her voice was simple, her eyes were clear. She just said it, the way she would have said water runs out of a tap, or the sun shines on the Thorn. Looking at her, he knew something all complete, all one piece, all of a sudden. What she was here to tell him was that she wanted to be his woman. It was the only thing she could be here for, and it was her way – the way he understood her way. It sure wasn't the way things were supposed to go between man and woman.

Now she was standing there, waiting. You could tell by looking at her, she figured the words she'd said were just as good as the words she'd been going to say. Now he was supposed to pick up on that. I mean, there she was, talking like that. Talking like that supposedly made her so good, no man like Jackson would even think before he took her up. I mean, hell, Honor, you're a strange one, and I'm a strange one, we don't stop to wonder does a strange one maybe seem strange to a strange one.

Ah, come on, he whispered to himself, you're looking for trouble. Been nothing but trouble all day – be just as sensible to figure you're due for a break.

But, yield, yield, he thought to himself, and the feeling came over him strong and hot that one of *us* at one time, on one day, for one killing, was enough.

'All right, then have this,' he said, jabbing the rolled-up drawing at her. 'You want to be different. That's different.'

She unrolled it and looked at it, and then looked up at him. 'You didn't make this up, did you? This is how it is.'

'Yeah. And now *you're* stuck with it.' He had no idea why he went on to say: 'By the way, my name's Jim.' He turned away and walked off, leaving her there.

Oh, people, Honor Secon Black Jackson thought. People. *People!*

II

It wasn't too crowded now. The farmers had gone off to the fields, and the women were doing their household stuff. The smell of fresh bread hung around the Thorn like glue. The Honors were either off sleeping or practising things. There were kids playing around, and some of them tried to hang on to him. But you can always get rid of a kid by looking at him as if he was nothing. Jackson did that as he walked along. Petra wouldn't have followed him; Petra wouldn't follow anybody. She'd wait. Or maybe she'd follow when no one was looking but she'd make it look like it was at her own good time.

Jackson walked over to the Thorn to look at his Amsir. He studied the places where it kept its wind and water stored inside itself, for piecing out to itself in the lonely ambushes of twilight. Looking at it that way, he could see how much it looked like a thin, dried-out man with big blisters under his skin. How much *he* looked like a thin, dried-out man. In his mind, Secon Jackson gave the Eld Honor another snort.

Red Filson grinned at him, rubbing his chin and jaw, which were as tough-looking as the rest of him. Secon Jackson knew his own face was flaming pink where the beard had been, and he didn't like to have Red Filson tell him he was funny-looking. But he wasn't that interested in Filson just now, and it probably showed, because Filson said: 'Just about everybody around the Thorn's gonna be at your feast tonight, huh? Spreadin' things a little thin.'

'Well, tell you – you're that worried, I'll watch this bird, and you go out and get another one to throw in the pot.'

Harrison chuckled softly. Filson never much changed expression. 'Some people figure they could maybe pay off everything the same day, I guess,' he said speculatively.

Jackson found himself having to look deep into Filson's eyes. 'Now and then, I guess, one day's all the time a man might need,' he said, thinking that one of the troubles with killing a man out in plain sight was you had to hang around for the Eld's judgement on you, and there was a lot of fasting, and of sitting around cogitating, and of trialling, to be got through. A man could sicken and die, waiting for the trialling to get over. He turned around and walked away, heading off between the nearest houses. And he just kept walking.

Chapter Six

I

It was hot and gritty, lying buried in the sand. Secon Jackson felt miserable. He lay trying to breathe as little as possible, just his nose out in sight, finding out about the world around him by ear. It had to be about a third of a dozen hours since he'd walked away from the Thorn. And lately he'd begun to hear stirrings in the ground – the *chucka-chucka-chucka* of quick-running feet, sometimes near and sometimes far. The sounds always moved from the direction of the Thorn, so he knew they weren't Amsirs. As a matter of fact, he was just far enough away from the Thorn to give trouble to anyone trying to find him, and not far enough out yet really to be in Amsir country.

He figured even with thirty or forty Honors to send out, the Eld would have a hell of a time finding him around the perimeter of as much radius as he had put between himself and the little concrete houses around the big metal spike.

He wasn't too worried about being found, both because there weren't enough people really to search and because whoever found him, he figured it would take more than one or two of them. Mostly, he lay there dreaming. There's a lot of stuff out here in the desert – spears, dead Honors, and very likely some dead Amsirs too, with holes from spear-wounded Honors in them, but no way for anybody to account for them in the village if the Honors couldn't come back. He dreamt about all those dead men under the sand with him. From the way the Eld had talked, things had been going the way they went now for a long time back. In that time a lot of metal spears and a lot of dead Honors must have got hidden out around here. If you could farm this well-fertilized country, the size of the javelin stalks you could raise!

But you can't raise a crop where you can't breathe, and if you're a farmer you only know one way to breathe. Well, Secon Jackson thought, come to that, if you're a Honor you only know one way to breathe. If you were a Amsir you probably didn't know any more than that. Oh, a man could find two, three different ways to get air and water, but that wasn't what he meant by that dream.

He didn't dare move much. He'd done a lot to cover his tracks and there was just enough constant rippling in the sand so that even when he wasn't hearing *chucka-chucka* sounds there was a sort of hissing in his ears. A dozen dozen dozen dozen grains of sand, he thought, dry as life, rubbing on each other. He saw himself floating in the sand, and the sand going on down deeper and deeper. He twitched a little finger and by the thickness of one grain of sand his finger hid itself farther. By the thickness of one grain of sand, pushing out of the way underneath, filling in above, he was that much closer to sinking down to where the deepness stopped. I could float, he thought, I could float here a long time, but I'd sink little by little.

What is this stuff I'm in? Dust. Nothing. Out at the edge of the fields, beyond the weed borders of the village, it smoked up into the air like hope and then twisted in around back on itself, drifting up so thin, so fine, that you could walk through it almost without knowing it was there, and could only see it edge-on when you were passing through the middle of it. Then it had substance; a thin, dirty yellow line, curving up in an arc that probably reached just below the gridwork at the top of the Thorn, but lost itself and couldn't be seen that high. Thin enough to drink.

Chucka-chucka-chucka. Someone was coming close, but off at a little bit of an angle. Secon Jackson judged it from the way the sounds didn't get louder quite as fast as they beat on the sand. Somebody running; some Honor saying to himself he would find Secon Jackson any minute now.

He wondered what the Eld was saying to the farmers to explain what had happened to Secon Jackson. He wondered if the Eld was bothering to say anything – they all knew Secon Jackson was crazy, or if they hadn't known it, it would occur to them now. He wondered what the Eld thought. It must be a good long time since a Honor ran out on his feast, a good long time since the Eld had seen any need to wonder what a man might be doing. Secon Jackson grinned carefully with the sand murmuring on his lips, and went on dreaming.

He dreamed through the rest of the short afternoon and into the twilight. When it was full dark and cold, and it had been three dozen parts of a day since he'd slept, he slipped up out of the sand. Boy, he thought, looking up at the night, I'd sure better know what I'm doing.

He began to walk towards the edge of the world. He felt a little draggy.

From time to time he put his face down to the ground, and from time to time he could hear the sound of running Honors, *chucka-chucka*ing distantly. Merely because they couldn't imagine what else to do, they were quartering back and forth across the line his Amsir had led him on yesterday. That happened to be exactly right, because that was where he was headed. He figured maybe Amsirs always worked back to that line in the end, when they'd got Honors far enough away from the Thorn. But he wasn't being any dumb Honor himself. For the time being he was headed off at another angle, covering more ground than you'd cover if you only had a used bubble of water and were planning ever to make it back to the Thorn.

He'd done that on purpose. He could imagine them comparing notes and figuring out he'd never gone to one of the Thorn taps. He could imagine them figuring out they couldn't figure out what the hell he'd been thinking of, just taking off like that. He had imagined them not believing it when he walked by first one line of huts, and then the next one farther out and then the next one and then out into the nearest field and then the one beyond that, and so on. They just couldn't believe it; when he was lost from sight of the people around the Thorn, covered by the houses between him and them, he could imagine them not believing he hadn't stopped just out of sight. But he'd done all that; he'd just sloped off and gone out without enough supplies, and he'd gone off without eating, and now he was headed in the wrong direction, and those were the only reasons he'd got away.

Well, no, Secon Jackson thought. He was going to get away because he could imagine them, but they couldn't imagine him. They could never imagine what he wanted. Come to that, he couldn't either. But he could move to it.

Red Filson's dart took him in the elbow.

It spun him around and knocked him down, and it took his left arm out of the fight. He sprang for his life, throwing himself off to one side, not even knowing yet whom he was fighting, knowing only because he rolled over its head that it was a dart in his elbow and not a spear.

Now the shock was going through him. It was so bad that even the back of his neck felt struck stiff. He'd never been clobbered so hard in his life. Then he saw the shape of the man-shadow jumping towards him. It was Filson. Lucky days, Jackson thought.

'Tough luck, Honor,' Filson said, getting ready to stab. He was very fast – as fast as Secon Jackson had ever dreamed him – and Jackson could only hope to be as fast as he had ever dreamed himself. He got out of the way of the first lunge, but he couldn't make his feet grip tight. When he tried to turn, his dead left arm knocked against his knee. He went down again, just as if Filson had struck him. It *was* like fighting in a dream.

Filson was good. He was like something you'd hear about from an old woman. Jackson flopped forward off his knees, knowing exactly how this would put him inside Filson's kick and knowing exactly what he would try to do to Filson after that. But Filson kicked him anyhow. And one more time Jackson was down.

He had his stick, but he didn't have either of his darts – the best he could do was grab his left wrist and scratch at Filson's side going by, using the head of the dart sticking out through his elbow. He might even have cut the other man some – he thought he'd felt the point dragging momentarily – but that was a hell of a defence to put up, wasn't it? He struck out at Filson with the stick, missing; dropped it, grabbed sand and threw it at the other man's face, and didn't seem to have any effect on him. 'Boy, you messed it,' Filson said. 'I would have figured you for my best enforcer when I became Eld. Your mother would have liked that a lot. Now look what you're doing to your family.'

Will they at least give me any peace in Ariwol? Secon Jackson thought as he twisted out of Filson's way again. He tried to think of things to do with one arm. He could pull off Red's cap, he supposed. But his own was loose and jouncing around his skull; he was in no shape for any game that two could play. He tried for a grip on Filson's dart-arm, but it was like trying to hold a piece of the Thorn come to life. The best he could do was drag his nails across Filson's biceps as the hold broke. He figured it would only take him two or three days to scratch the man to death.

He spun away and tried to drag the dart out of his elbow so that he would have a weapon too, but all that did for him was nearly make him faint.

They were scuffling and fluttering like two kids under a blanket out here; whirling and groping for each other in the dark, raising dust, making slapping sounds as they tried for each other and made each other miss. But it couldn't be much longer before Filson got that other dart in. Jackson knew it, and Filson knew it. Filson was doing it like a practice. He even found time to talk. 'Where did you think you were going?' he panted. 'It's all right being crazy, but I never figured you for dumb.'

Maybe he thought that would be a finish line. His arm hooked down and came up again, and his forearm snapped over as he punched his dart towards Jackson's face. Jackson dropped under it, but he was off his feet again. He made a try at knocking Filson's knees together, and then dropped sideways, barely getting out of the way of the other man's return stroke. The side of Jackson's face was in the sand.

That made all the difference. He could hear the new sounds coming up fast . . . *chicka-sip, chicka-sip, chicka-sip.*

In his mind – but very quickly – Secon Jackson laughed like crazy. It was working out after all. Turned out he'd damned near died before he could know for sure. Maybe he still would, if he couldn't stall Red off.

He had to interrupt himself to flounder out of the way of the next rush.

But it was nice to know he'd been figuring it all correct, from the minute that he had been sitting there in the Eld's room in the Thorn and had been beginning to think on it, because where else was there any hope for him.

He pushed the laugh out into the cold air. 'Huh!' He kicked towards Red's ankle and made him hop back. 'I know where I'm goin'.' Well, no, he didn't, but he knew whom he was going with. *Chicka-sip, chicka-sip, chicka-sip, whop!* That was the sound of the running Amsir coming down solid on both feet nearby. Up against the stars and the horizon there was a fast glimpse, for Jackson to get, of a javelined wing unfurling.

'I yield! I yield!' Jackson shouted to the Amsir, making a grab for Red, who was distracted. His two stiff fingers hooked upwards into Filson's nostrils. His arm pulled back hard, and at the same time he planted one foot and kicked Filson in the crotch. Filson bent double, with both his hands still clapped to his torn, shocked face. Jackson plucked Filson's second dart from between the man's limp fingers and then made one move more, with the dart held for cutting windows. He dropped the dart and stood holding his right thumb and forefinger tight around his left arm above the elbow. The Amsir stood looking at him, its spear ready, only the lace stirring on its body.

'I do yield,' Jackson said, looking down at Filson all huddled up. He kicked a little sand towards the dead man. 'My name is Honor Red Jackson.'

II

'You will come with me, wet devil?' the Amsir said in its high, puzzled voice. You could tell it – he felt proud, but you could tell he couldn't understand what had happened. Well, that was all right, too, Jackson thought.

'I better had,' Jackson said. 'Or there's been a lot done for nothing. My mother's a widow twice over for nothing.'

'You're wounded, devil. You're spilling moisture. Come with me quickly.'

'Right behind you.'

'Before me.'

They ran over the night desert, *chucka-chucka-chucka, chicka-sip, chicka-sip.* The Amsir gave Jackson his directions with light little touches of the spearpoint, until finally they reached the place the Amsir wanted, and the leathery bird said: 'Stop. Dig here.'

Crouching down, Jackson did his one-handed best. A sixth of a dozen feet down, he felt something hard and swollen under his fingertips. He pulled it out. It was a bladder of some kind, twice as thick through as a man's head. It felt as if it were made of glue-varnished leather; he could feel the edges of seams, and then a folded-in gut stopper.

'That is breathing-stuff,' the Amsir said. 'You will need it soon; the iron cap is almost useless to you now. Dig deeper – there is a moisture-bottle, and there are wrappings for warmth. There are patches for your hide.'

Jackson dug them out. The water bottle was a lot like the Amsir-bubble at his back in size, but it felt like the oxygen bladder. The robes were some kind of leather, tanned soft. They'd used leather for the body-patches, too. They thought of everything when they cached one of these bringing-in-the-prisoner kits; they knew they weren't likely to get many without holes in them.

He still couldn't get the dart out, so he tied off his arm, using his good hand and his teeth to make the knot. The Amsir wouldn't come anywhere nearer him than the length of the spear.

There were sling-straps for the oxygen bladder and water bottle. He unhooked his own bubble, drained it dry, and tossed it away in the dark before he replaced it with the Amsir bottle. Then he said: 'Set,' and they began moving again towards where once upon a time his incurving horizon had been.

As they travelled, he asked: 'You bring in any other prisoners in your time?'

'You're my first.'

We sure have lost a lot of maidens today, Jackson thought. He was getting very cold. After a while, he had to pull out the length of tied-off intestine into the oxygen bubble, stick the end of it in his mouth, and use that for air, pinching the gut between two fingers to keep himself from swelling into broken-lunged sickness and death, as the Amsir warned him.

When the sun came up, they saw it sooner than almost anybody Jackson knew, for they were at the top of his world's rim.

Jackson was bone-pulling cold. He had to peek out between his eyelids. He hurt in his nose and his ears, and behind his ears. He saw his robes were made of stitched-together human skins, and for a minute he was scared and furious, but then he remembered the thrown-away Amsir-bubble, and he told himself it didn't mean much. Or maybe it did, but not now.

'Hurry along; you will die here, but it is not much farther to comfort . . . of a kind.'

Jackson squinted ahead. He saw below him another great dish-shaped world. But this one was blue-green from rim to rim; fences, light as stretched strings marking out plots, divided the land. High houses on stilt legs shone pink and ochre and glistening blue; bright yellow and sharp green, flashing in the sunlight. Lacy lines, fragile as the fencing, traced from house to house, swaying down in free arcs, webbing the whole town together. And at the centre of this world, far away, he could see a Thorn. A tall, massive, shining Thorn, not the blunt, tilted, rust-streaked thing he had been born under. A fairy trap of gridwork twined in the air around its peak. And everywhere, everywhere, in the air, curving, curvetting, disporting, the Amsirs trafficked with the early-morning air.

Air. Thick, lustrously clear, it reached out to envelop him as the Amsir pushed him forward.

Ariwol! Jackson thought, Ariwol, by all that's pious! He arched his back and stared up into the sky again. Shouting and singing and laughing, he thought: But I don't see you, Red.

Chapter Seven

I

'You will have to climb down,' the Amsir said, showing Jackson a place on the rim where you could see something that looked a little like a path. 'You can leave those things here. They will be taken.'

Jackson dropped the stuff on the ground, and when the Amsir negligently knocked his spearpoint against the iron cap, Jackson took that off too and set it down on top of the pile. All he had left now was the dart still trapped in the joint of his left elbow, and the human leather tourniquet. He shrugged and began to scramble down. It was six or eight times his own height to the ground.

The Amsir did something that must have given him a lot of pleasure. He stepped off a steep place in the rim, cupped his wings, and pivoted luxuriantly so as to be able to keep watching Jackson while he drifted downwards. Every so often he beat his wings once or twice gracefully and kept himself from sinking too quickly.

For Jackson, climbing down wasn't any picnic. He had to do it all one-handed, which meant that often enough he had to brace himself by leaning his face or his chest into the broken grit so as to help keep his feet from sliding. It was just too damn bad, wasn't it?

He began running into patches of the pretty blue-green stuff that he had seen filling the bottom of this world so attractively right up to the rim. It was cheesey and brittle. It broke off and smeared on his hand and body when he rubbed against rocks it was growing on. It smelled sharp, the way old bread dough tasted, and it came apart in little leafy chips. Jackson had never seen anything like it before. While it had looked fine from up there on the rim, down here it looked a little bit like something that had made somebody sick.

He got down to flat land with a half-twist of his body that left him leaning against the rocks at the bottom of the rim.

From down here it was only a gentle slope for maybe a dozen strides, and then everything flattened out. Already, from this angle, most of his view of the Amsir Thorn was blocked by the Amsir houses stilting their way into the air. It all looked different, not as spread out, and pretty crowded.

His left forearm and hand were turning purplish white. The Amsir came down lightly a few strides away from him as he stopped to loosen the tie above his elbow, and leaned watching the blood squirt out around the dart. He tried to work his fingers. Finally he reached over with his right hand and pushed against the crooked stiffness in his fingers. A little bit of that and he was able to make his thumb and forefinger twitch towards each other. They were also beginning to feel like he was holding them in a fire. Give and take. He tied the leather band tight again.

The Amsir said curiously: 'How long will that take to heal?'

'I don't know. Long time, I guess. Tell you better after somebody helps me get this dart out.'

'We have people who can do that. But I don't mean how long until it is perfect; in your experience how long until it can do work?'

'Look, I don't know. Six, nine days. Maybe twelve. Maybe three.'

'Three . . .' the Amsir repeated to himself thoughtfully, He looked Jackson up and down. 'No sooner?'

'Look, I *told* you – ' Jackson stopped and let it go. People never believed anything they hadn't touched, and the Amsir didn't have any dart in his elbow. The Amsir was just standing there with his lace drifting perkily around him in the breeze that swept towards the rim along the floor of the world and vanished up the rocks. Jackson knew there was something different about his face, and then he saw that there were two wrinkle-edged holes open there, where a man's nostrils would be if his upper lip was an Amsir beak. And he could hear air hissing in and out. The Amsir was upwind of him, too, and now that he noticed, Jackson could smell the old breath emptying itself out of his chest bubbles.

'Come along,' the Amsir said, motioning with his spear.

'We don't have time to waste. You have to walk to the tower.' He pointed with one wing tip. By that Jackson could tell he meant the Thorn. 'You'll have to just walk through the fields,' the Amsir said as he sprang up into the air to circle watchfully around Jackson. 'We don't make paths.'

You don't take many prisoners, Jackson thought. It's a big day.

They stopped briefly once, at the nearest of the stilt-legged houses. The house was made of something tough like horn, but scratched up and very old, looking as if it had once held a lot more particles of its bright yellow colour. The Amsir sprang higher into the air and clung to one of the uprights with his claws and one hand. He reached up over his head to tug on the downswinging loop of the line that connected this house to the next one. Jackson could hear a bell clang inside. Clang, long pause, clang clang, short pause, then more clangs and spaced-out pauses.

It got mixed up in Jackson's ears. As soon as the line had transmitted the Amsir's pulling up to the next house, he could hear another bell in there echoing the sound. Then he could hear it again faintly from the house beyond that, and then very faintly off in the distance, always moving in the direction of the Thorn. The Amsir stopped pulling and waited. After a little while, Jackson could hear a sound coming back along the ropes from the direction of the Thorn. It was a short answer, whatever it was. The Amsir nodded in satisfaction and waved Jackson on with his spear.

'All right, hurry up, now,' he cried down. 'They are waiting for you.'

They were getting notice from other Amsirs now, too. Some of them popped out of the doorways of the houses, jumping into the air and swooping to get a look at Jackson. Others – women and young kids, or anyway acting like women and young kids would have acted if they'd been farmers – clinging to the edges of doorways.

It began to make something of a procession, Jackson down below and all the inhabitants overhead. The Amsirs called to each other and back to their families in their homes. And the families back to them. It made a hell of a racket in the air, and shadows and gusts down on the ground. Jackson tried baffling them a little by walking under the houses instead of around them, but there was too much manure on the ground there, and he didn't try it twice. He walked along with his head down, holding his arm out of his way, humming a little song his mother had taught him and had liked to hear him sing:

'Ah, when I am a Honor,/And go for my game,/The people of dirt will report my new name./The Eld he will shave me/And name my new name/And the people of iron will feast on my game./The beasts of the sand/Will grow fearful and tame./The Honor of iron will have a new name! CHORUS: *'Talordims zasheparda/Ishalna twan . . ./Talordims zasheparda/Ishalna twan!'*

By the time he got to the foot of their Thorn, the Amsirs were worked up nearly out of their minds; with the crying and the calling, and the flurry of wings, he could have thrown his head back and hollered at the top of his lungs, and who would have heard? Exactly. Who would have heard? Humming was good enough for him, and, besides, he was disgusted with the way they were behaving.

There were guards and things at the entrance to the Thorn, hooting and shaking their spears in deference to his particular Amsir's dignity as a bringer-in of people. There were thumping, rustling crowds of Amsirs jumping down out of the air and mobbing around behind him and his Amsir, pressing forward towards the entrance. But only Jackson and his Amsir got let through the doorway, which got swung shut behind them, leaving the two of them standing there in silence, before Jackson got hustled forward again, and up a corridor towards a room where they were being waited for. It certainly was suddenly quiet. He was given a nudge into the room, and besides other Amsirs of various sizes and kinds, there was one who crouched and turned his head on a bent neck.

'You'll find us quicker than your kind. What do I call you?' this one said. '"Wet devil" is too respectful, and "Man" is ambiguous. What's your personal handle?' Well, if he wasn't their Eld, he would do.

11

'My name's Honor Red Jackson,' he said to the crouching old Amsir. Maybe not too old. Crouching wasn't right, either – it was more like leaning bent-legged, with some of his weight on his wing tips.

'They have a complex system of naming,' quickly said another old, skinnier Amsir. There were quite a few Amsirs in the room, including a doctor-like one. That one stepped forward and began peering at his elbow. Then he began studying it, in part by twisting the naked dry human arm bones he'd been holding in one hand. Jackson hoped he'd soon figure out just how he was going to tinker this thing up, and get around to doing his job.

'Honor is his community status,' the skinny one was still explaining. 'It signifies that he lives exclusively by hunting our sort of creature. Red means that in addition to having met the hunting requirement, he has also performed the optional office of killing a creature of his own kind. Jackson simply means he is the son of another male creature named Jack. For creatures in sparse circumstances, they have a most amazing variety of rituals. I can't imagine how they distinguish between brothers of identical status – I do not say they don't so distinguish. I'm sure they do.'

The Amsir Eld grunted at the skinny one. 'Do not, I pray, give me any more labels for him. They may have to distinguish, but we never have so many of them that we must. Tell me what he is, not what he stands for.'

'I am telling you. It's significant that he should be so obviously young; that he should carry the very fresh scars of combat with one of our kind – which means he brought one of our kind to the last extremity – and then the even more recent scars of combat with one of his own kind. This was an odd one, even before he did the oddest thing of all and yielded voluntarily.' The skinny Amsir looked at Jackson proudly, as if he'd produced him himself.

'The odder the better,' the Eld Amsir snapped. 'We've had no luck with the usual run.'

'Precisely my point,' the instructing Amsir said.

'Then why didn't you make it to begin with?'

'Pfah! I did!'

'Only in hindsight. Get out. Wait where you're needed.' The Eld Amsir jerked his head towards the doorway and the instructor shuffled out. The Eld Amsir turned all his attention towards Jackson's end of the room. 'You, Doctor – get on with it.' He came a few steps closer and he wasn't old, now that he was in some kind of better light coming in through the narrow Thorn window-slits. The tattering of his lace, and the crumpled look of the wing Jackson could see best, were accounted for by damage. He was pretty badly scarred up, and discoloured. He looked as if he'd been picked up and knocked hard against something rough, had left big patches of his hide against that rough thing, and had had a lot of bones broken for it. But he threw his weight around like an Eld, and that bothered Jackson. He didn't like the idea of somebody being mean enough inside to be an Eld, but still not slowed down in his head very much.

'You, Jackson – I am above all others here. No one of my kind of creature will tell you we have any time, so give me straight, fast answers. The report is you were ready to yield when that young one by the doorway found you. This is something new. Explain it.'

The doctor put one hand on Jackson's biceps, the other on his forearm and closed his beak on the lace-feathered end of the dart in Jackson's elbow. His claws made little purchase-hunting sounds on the metal flooring.

Jackson figured it would be best to pay him no heed. 'Didn't like it where I was,' he said to the Eld. 'Figured I'd go to where the lies were all about. Make up my own if I had to.'

'Pfu. Lies require life. You won't live.'

'Right up to the minute I die, I will. Oh, hell!' he hollered as the doctor jerked his head back while twisting his arm. The dart sucked out of Jackson's wound and hung for an instant in the doctor's beak until it was dropped. The doctor's hand closed as best it could above Jackson's elbow – the fingers couldn't make it all the way around the flesh. Jackson reached over to help him, his eyes swimming.

'I think perhaps you thought you could hunt us as we hunt you,' the Eld said shrewdly. 'I think perhaps you thought out that there was another world in which our sort of creature was prey. I think you thought you knew a way to get breathing stuff. You are young. Your judgements are romantic. You thought that because you were a little bit odd, and you frightened your own kind, you would frighten us too.'

Jackson just kept gripping his arm, swaying with his eyes closed. He did have room enough inside himself, though, to think how wonderful it was that *everybody*, Amsirs included, could think they knew everything just because they knew something.

'Well, that's not how it is, creature,' the Eld Amsir went right on, while the doctor unstoppered a stone bottle of something that looked like water but burned like fire when he poured it over Jackson's running elbow, and then began winding a long, tight strip of shaved-thin hide around Jackson's left arm in a spiral from shoulder to wrist. 'In some ways here for you it is the way it is for our kind of creature with you. We cannot breathe the breathing stuff around your fields. Muck from that stuff you grow is in every breathful. We die – you would say prettily – with our first breath of it; our muscles knot so hard our bones break; our backbones snap; green fur fills our lungs. Or so the instructors say, from the times long ago when we still tried.

'Haw! We die of breathing the air that blows across the stuff you eat. *This* is the stuff we eat.' He pointed a wing at a corner heaped with the blue, crumbly stuff from the fields. 'That is rock-stuff. That is the food for creatures of wing and spirit. Can you eat rock? No others of your kind have ever been able to. You will die, prettily. Your stomach will sink in, your bones will show through the meat on you; towards the end, you will try to fang us and we will kick you away. You will bite yourself. You will try to get away to your poison Thorn, and we will kick you back to your work.

You will live altogether perhaps thirty days, perhaps less. Only *perhaps* perhaps will you live any *long*er than that. And only perhaps perhaps perhaps will you ever be happy again before you die. It depends how quickly and how well you can do things. On how odd you are, and most of all on whether you are luckier than any other creature of your own kind that we have ever had here. Now – ' he jerked his head towards Jackson's bound-up arm. 'How soon do you think you will be able to do work with that?'

Jackson raised his arm experimentally. It throbbed when he did that; it felt like something made out of one solid stick of bone. 'Thanks, Doc,' he said to the doctor, who was standing off to one side watching him critically. Jackson tried to make his hand work. It wouldn't work. He began knocking it against his thigh, trying to get some circulation into his fingers. 'What kind of work?' he said to the Eld Amsir.

'I'll show you.' The Eld gestured towards the doorway. 'Turn towards your right hand after you leave the room.'

III

Jackson did that. The Eld Amsir and the young one who'd brought him followed him. The doctor tried to go with him too, but the Eld just looked back over his shoulder and said 'Not you.' The doctor turned around quickly, and rustled out towards the daylight Jackson had come from.

The way Jackson had been told to turn led him deeper into the Amsir Thorn. It was a narrow passageway, and at widely-spaced distances there were lights glowing behind translucent panels in the metal ceiling overhead. It was like walking through something's ribs; every so often they'd come to another oval ridge that ran completely around, up the walls and across the ceiling. There was always an open door folded neatly back against the wall. Halfway between two of these doors there'd be another one like it, but set directly into the wall at Jackson's left side. These were closed; sometimes there was light behind them, coming through a little bull's-eye window, and sometimes there wasn't. Sometimes there were particular sounds of machines going; sometimes there was just a general sound of the Thorn, which was louder and healthier than Jackson's Thorn. But not one of these doors leading to the inside told him anything.

The passageway curved this way and that; sometimes it turned sharply. From the sound growing louder and louder, and then beginning to taper off behind him at more or less the same rate, Jackson guessed it was some kind of path they'd set up for getting through the Thorn to the other side without having to go around it. Three times they came to ladders taking up half the passageway's space and going up to round doors set in the ceiling. Two of them were closed, and the metal rungs of the ladders were dull and softly smooth. At the top of the third ladder was a round black opening, and the ladder was scratched up. There were bright, polished places on the wall, going up beside the ladder, where Amsir wings had dragged against it a lot of times. He tried to imagine an Amsir working his way up one of these ladders, just as he could see how they had to inch and shuffle to get around the ladders and keep going down the passageway. It wasn't handy for them, this place. Well, it wasn't handy for him either, but it was what they had.

They came to another room that opened outside. It had a couple more Amsirs in it; a plump young one, and the instructor, again.

'Are you going to show it to him now?' this one asked the Eld.

'He won't get any stronger.'

'No – or at least, none of them have. But you know, they do have this ability to store energy. Amazing really, when you think of it; at least, we've never observed any of them taking nourishment out into the desert with them, and we know they've certainly been able to function unfed for significant periods of time here. Whereas we're hard put to it to find individuals with the endurance to omit feeding for as much as a day –'

'– What the learned one who is well above me refers to,' broke in the instructor's young Amsir, 'is the surmise that perhaps these creatures are trading time for energy. They may be going into some sort of survival mode that permits a stretch-out of energy consumption by maintaining a low level of physical and mental activity. As you know from the learned one's witnessed discourses, he would very much like to attempt stimulating one of these creatures, as for example with pain, on the supposition that this may force it to re-enter a more energetic mode, of shorter duration, perhaps, but much more productive of over-all results . . .'

Nobody listened with interest. Not even the instructor Amsir, who was doing his best not to pay attention, or at least to look as if he were someplace else entirely. He looked at the walls, the floor, and the ceiling while the novice instructor's voice got lower and lower. Jackson didn't want to hear anything about pain, whatever a mode was. The young Amsir who'd brought him in was looking at the instructor novice the way a Honor would look at a farmer his own age, except he wasn't measuring him for the kill. Finally, the Eld Amsir said 'Shut up,' gently, and the novice instructor did. Looking at Jackson the Eld Amsir said 'Do the young practise as much where you come from?'

'Only honning. The farming takes care of itself; the Thorn spreads the water in the fields, and the ploughs run straight no matter what you try to do.'

'Well, we are better than you,' the Eld said. 'Both of you shut up,' he added towards the instructor, who'd begun to open his beak. 'This one's enough experiment for me just the way he is.' He nudged Jackson towards the door with the tip of one wing. 'Step out and look at that,' he said.

Jackson found himself looking from the doorway at something a lot like a small Thorn. It tapered up into the air, maybe a dozen times as high as a man. But it was spikier, and it had other spikes curving down – it rested on three of them. It had openings, too, like throats yawning down towards the ground. It was made of the same kind of metal as the Thorn; in that shape, though, spiky and open-mouthed, it looked mean and twisty.

'What is that?' Jackson asked.

'It's the Object. It's been here since the beginning of the world. You see that?' the Eld pointed up the side of the thing. There was a ladder coming down to within, say, three feet of the ground. Jackson squinted; up at the head of the ladder was something that looked like another one of the closed doorways, but that had no familiar circular handle to turn. It was just an oval crack in the metal. Turning his head, and shifting his feet back and forth, Jackson could see glints from scratches up there; shallow ones, it looked like, no more than futile scrapes.

'That's a doorway, isn't it?' the Eld Amsir said.

'Looks like one,' Jackson agreed. 'Don't you know?'

'It says it's a doorway. It has a voice, and the instructor tells me that's what it says.' The Eld cast a glance aside at the instructor: 'There isn't anyone who will tell me it says something else,' he added dryly.

'I've spent a long time deciding that's what it says,' the instructing Amsir said vehemently. 'I have given witnessed discourses – '

'Shut up,' the Eld Amsir said.

Jackson looked the Object up and down again. There wasn't anything new left to notice, except maybe for the burnt, black splashes on the ground right under it, that the spikey legs rested on. That looked a little wrong – as if somebody had been building fires under it not too long ago; certainly not as long ago as the beginning of time. Otherwise, it just sat there. He certainly didn't hear any voice saying 'I am a door.'

'What do you want me to do with this thing?'

'Climb the ladder and open the door,' the Eld Amsir said.

'Just that?'

'*Pfu!* Every one of our kind of creature who's tried it has been killed . . . except for a very few of us who have only been hurt and made very angry. And too wise to try again. Every one of your kind of creature who's tried it has failed. But he hasn't been killed. He's had plenty of time to try anything he pleases, until he's finally starved to death.'

Chapter Eight

I

Oh, haw, Jackson thought, feeling weak and disgusted. He looked up towards the door in the Object again, and then at the ladder. It seemed to him that a bone-weary, one-armed, light-headed, sleepless, foodless, hopeless man could get up it all right. Considering everything. He looked at the door again. But the damn thing didn't have any handle. Well. He got himself moving and sauntered towards the ladder.

Standing there right under the Object, he could see two things; one, that it was pretty big, the other that it had been there long enough for the three spikes it rested on to have become very nearly a part of the soil. It no longer looked as if it had been set down on the ground. It had the look that the walls of the huts at the home Thorn had – or that the Thorn itself had, come to that – of having poked up from underneath, and of the ground bulging just a little bit at the torn edges, as if maybe a dozen years from now it would finish reacting to this growth and would finally lie flat.

He put his good hand on the ladder two or three rungs up. He gave a little tug followed by a harder one. There was no give in the ladder. He could see that it came out of the side of the Object, up there just below the doorway. And he could see a sort of joint at each rung, as if the ladder were made to be pulled up and to fold inside a small space somewhere up there. Or to be kicked out and let hang this way when needed. But if those were hinges, they had no give in them now. He put his ear to the ladder, which was as warm as his own flesh, and he could hear things humming. Well, anything that could talk had to have a heart.

He looked over at the bunch of Amsirs. All of them were watching him with considerable interest. There were other Amsirs gathering overhead – passers-by and just loungers who'd noticed that a new creature of his kind was about to try for the talking door.

One of them swooped down and came no more than his own height over Jackson's head. 'Haa, Wet Devil! Climb! Climb!' He hovered up at the level of the door and made scrabbling fake-desperate grabs towards it for as long as he could hold his altitude, then fell away, got his wings straightened back around the way he wanted them, and buffeted up into the air again. Jackson noticed that it would have been a much better piece of mockery if the Amsir had dared actually to touch the door. Jackson took a little jump into the air, grabbed the ladder, got one foot up, and began to climb.

It was peculiar the way the metal felt neither cold nor hot. Although he had to do all the work with one arm and his legs, it was nothing like when he'd had to slip and slide down the rim into this place. He felt pretty good, as a matter of fact. There were worse things a man could do with his time than climb this ladder. He wished he knew what the Object was.

Pretty soon he was up high enough to look down at the Amsirs on the ground. They were all watching him, their faces turning up, gridwork-like, to follow his climb as if each of their bodies were a Thorn and he was the sun.

Up to now, the ladder had been hanging reasonably far away from the side of the Object. But the higher he got, the closer the bulge of the Object got to the straight-hanging ladder. Now his eyes were only inches away from the side of the thing itself, and he could see something that didn't cheer him up. It was grease-smears, rainbowing in the light, from all the hands that had rubbed here before him as he stopped to lean his weight on the comfortable, neither warm nor cold humming metal.

Oh, pfu, he said to himself, and kept climbing, until finally he was at the top of the ladder. Here there was a little open door, not too thick, but not too thin, and strongly hinged, positioned under the slits so as to protect it against anything being thrown up from below. When the ladder was pulled up, probably the little door closed behind it and left no more seam than the door above it did. When his eyes came level with it, he noticed that there was a broken-off, fleshless fingerbone trapped in the crack between the little open door and the main side of the Object. At the same time, a voice over his head growled hollowly: 'Ouwwtenshownnn. Dhayss dwuuhrr uhhpnnss owwnnuhhli t umm-nn pehrrowwnnuhll. Awwll ouwwthrr uhluff-ffouwrrmms wuull be dhaysstroydd wieyethouyut dhaysscriyeshunn.'

Jackson looked up at the door. Nothing was happening. The door began to say again: 'Ouwwtenshownnn. Dhayss dwuuhrr . . .'

Jackson climbed back down the ladder.

'Shakes you, doesn't it?' said the Eld Amsir, at the foot of the ladder.

'It sounds like somebody's stomach,' Jackson said. He looked over at the instructing Amsir. '*What* did he say it says?' The Eld followed his glance and raised a wing tip. The instructor Amsir came forward, brimming over and ready to spill.

'Do not be misled by the growling, rumbling, sounds. I have said them to myself at any number of speeds and pitches of voice, and I have had many below me say them to me in various modes according to my instructions. I have had witnesses in great number judge the various effects, and arrive at agreement among themselves as to the meaning of this sort of speech. It is the consensus,' he said with proud conclusiveness, 'that what the door is giving is first of all a sound much like our word "Display alertness". This is followed by a sound which is very definitely the word "object". Then there is a sound very much like our word "hatch" – '

'Shut up,' Jackson said to the shock of some, and the amusement of the Eld. 'You mean that's just a funny way of talking straight.'

The instructing Amsir looked at Jackson almost tearfully, as if it were a farmer whose daughter had just gone off with a Honor, laughing. 'That's right.'

'I want to get this straight. It talks like we do but it has a funny mouth, is that it?'

'That seems to be the case,' the Eld Amsir said.

'Well, now look,' Jackson said. 'That's a big thing. There's your kind of creature and my kind of creature, and now all of a sudden there's a third kind. And if it's all connected up with things that have been here since the beginning of time, then it could be that this thing talks for whatever made time begin. Maybe it *is* whatever made time begin.'

'Listen, you stinking wet – You keep *your* mouth off theology!'

The young Amsir who'd brought him in had been hanging around all this time, without saying two words or even boo. It made Jackson twang a little inside, having him come on this strong all of a sudden. But he rolled his eyes over at the youngster with enough cool to make it stick. 'Now what are *you* talking about?'

'Don't pick at it,' the Eld Amsir said to the young warrior. Saying it that way was maybe the fond substitute for 'Shut up!'. 'It's just an ignorant creature. Listen, I think things are pretty well controlled here – you can go home and tell your flock you are well above many for this day's work. Go home. Now.'

The young Amsir jumped for the air. 'I am rewarded,' he said thankfully to the Eld, before he flung himself straight up like a thrown dart aimed at the sun, shouting at the top of his lungs 'I am above many! I am above many!' High, high up, he flung himself out flat and went tearing down at a shallow angle for a particular one of the stilt-legged houses, still shouting. Jackson could hear his voice shrinking into the distance for a long time.

The Eld Amsir looked at Jackson and shrugged. 'You have one or two things to watch out for besides the condition of your stomach. One of them is the fact that if you nudge superstition hard enough around here, you won't live to starve. And there's not much chance any of the few enlightened persons will be able to do anything to help you.'

'We have a very tricky situation going here,' the instructor Amsir explained. 'You see, we know there are two Thorns, two worlds, two kinds of creature, and we know they were all made at the same time. One must be good, and the other evil. But you see, beyond that point we leave rational logic behind, and begin trespassing on matters of faith.

'A great prophet, one of whose last discourses I myself was

privileged to witness as a very young man, tells us that since we must make valuations of our Thorn's worth on faith, then it is just as logical to believe that each individual makes either good or evil of his own place. But for this the great prophet was flung from a great height with his wings broken, by those who avoid such complicated patterns of ethics. The simple view consists of knowing that it is our place that is good and yours that is evil, and that the mob are therefore good, for living in the good place.

'We, speaking together here, are all reasonable creatures – granting you a certain shrewdness. Being reasonable, we know it is probably only an accident of creation that your kind of creatures and mine cannot live in each other's places. But you see how difficult it could be to perceive that this one is of a tender and uncultured turn of mind.'

'You can see, too,' the Eld Amsir added, 'how brave that young fellow was, being as emotional as he is, and yet willing to risk waiting around the fringes of your world for something as unutterably evil and repulsive as yourself to come into contact with him. That's besides the risk of death – but then, no one really believes in death.' The Eld looked at Jackson significantly.

Jackson just looked back at him. For one thing, he didn't even know what 'theology' meant. It was the apprentice instructor who said: 'Look at him! He shows no sign of understanding! I propose the thesis they have no concept of original evil!'

'And are therefore innocent?' the instructor cried furiously. 'Shut up! Shut up!' He waved his wings, spastically hopping from one foot to the other, raising dust. He was pretty old and stiff, and didn't impress Jackson much, but the apprentice instructor quailed and ducked away, his head bowed. He acted as if he'd fallen out while running around the Thorn behind Red Filson – tireless, wise, dead Red Filson. What makes you dumb, Jackson decided, is what scares you.

II

'You see,' the Eld Amsir said to Jackson, 'we do feel we must discover whatever is within the Object. We feel this with different degrees of involvement.' He glanced aside at the instructor, who was busily running his fingertips through his lace and getting it untangled. 'Feel it for different reasons that are very close to our emotions. But it's our only clue to the nature and purpose of Creation. We've studied the Thorn for generations, of course, but it's only a machine. All we learn from it is how it works and in what parts it seems to be wearing out. It does seem to be wearing out in a number of parts. Now the Object, on the other hand, talks. Perhaps there is something inside. Perhaps one could talk to the inside something, with the right kind of mouth.'

'In what kind of talk?' Jackson asked.

The Eld Amsir nodded. 'Well remarked. Nobody is saying there won't be problems. Nobody is saying the answer will be easy to find. But we've got to begin. Things are not getting any better. They can only get worse. We can't just let them go. Oh, there are many of our kind of people who would never care, until the last moment when the sky fell down upon them. All they care about is getting their food to eat, water to drink, room to fly. And there have always been these things, so they can't imagine they could end. But we know the Thorn can end. So these things can end – there can be a last day for this world.

'There are some of us who cannot live content, knowing this, even though we may also know that we will be able to die content long before it becomes necessary to really have the answers we seek. There is a certain quirk – a restlessness, in certain minds, which does not seem to understand the passage of time. What will be real someday to everyone is very real to them now.'

Jackson listened politely.

'Now, I bear you no malice, boy. If we had food here that you could eat, I would give it to you – provided. Provided

I thought you would work just as hard at opening the door as you would if you were starving. Others may bear you malice, but I don't. I understand that we are really very much alike inside. And I like the idea of your being an odd one. I am an odd one too, among my own kind.' He pointed towards the Object. 'That's where I was mangled.

'I wouldn't leave it alone. I tried to crawl up one of its throats, but I was clumsy. As all of us who don't need the ground all our lives are clumsy when we crawl. My clumsiness saved my life. I fell to the ground. Fire burst forth from the throat, to clear me out, I suppose. But I was already crawling away. Still, it caught and threw me a good distance. Haw, they called it the reward for foolishness. I lay there screaming, and they gathered around laughing and exclaiming. That's when I understood I must either rule them or not live here any longer.

'I owe a good deal to the Object. I owe a good deal to being odd. And I tell you, odd one, that you'd better owe much to it, too.

'I'll do whatever needs to be done to force the most out of you. I will remind you, if you haven't thought of it yourself already, that it treats your kind of creature better than it treats my kind. My kind can't climb the ladder to its top, nor touch the door. When we try, something goes into my kind of creature from the door, flattens its insides, boils its eyes, throws it dead instantly earthward. Your kind of creature it merely permits to starve while attempting to crawl through the throat, or while picking at the door seam.'

The Eld grunted painfully. 'There's another thing. Let it give you hope. If the Object was made with the Thorn when time began, it was made, like the Thorn, for creatures with your kind of body.' The Eld glanced briefly at the places where the three-fingered hands grew out of his wings. 'Therefore, what's inside and makes that noise will probably not treat you like an enemy. It may help you. Why not believe there's your sort of food in there? What's a friend for, if not to offer hospitality? And I think you'll do well. You're very much like me, and if my body were like yours, I think I would do well.'

I'll bet you do think that, Jackson thought. He said: 'You know, I think you're right about how much alike our kinds of creature are. There's somebody who lives in our Thorn that I think you could spend a lot of happy hours with. Just talking. Comparing problems. Sharing thoughts.'

But the Amsir Eld didn't seem to understand. He looked at Jackson the way Jackson looked at people who used words like *theology*. Well, Jackson decided, it was possible to talk, talk, talk about how alike they were under the skin, but if you had become the Eld of the Amsirs, you couldn't really think there was anyone else who'd made out as wonderfully as you.

The way, when I was a kid, Jackson thought, I thought there was only one world, and the only thing in it was honning. He looked around at the Amsirs, the blue food he couldn't eat, the stilty houses, the sky filled with flapping creatures, and the Object. And I wish, he thought, I wish I was still like those farmers and Honors back there who still think that's all there is.

He felt pretty tired. 'I'm going to get some sleep,' he said, lay down, curled up, and closed his eyes around the throbbing of his arm.

III

Wow, his arm hurt. He scraped his eyes open and looked down at it. The flesh of his hand was swollen up in a doughy ring around the lower edge of the wrapping. When he reached up to touch his shoulder he found another bulge like it there. He rolled over in the dust near the object, rubbed his hair and face, pawed his open mouth, licked his teeth. He saw it was morning again. His skin felt dry. He couldn't get his face to work. He sat up, and saw the Amsir Eld sitting there. 'Huh! Been guarding my rest?'

'Mine, too. I've been wondering what effect a long rest would have on your energy supply. You don't seem to have become any more alert.'

Jackson moved. He had it pretty well planned, the next

step was to get around behind the Eld, hook his arms under the Eld's wings, whatever good the left arm might do, and get his right thumb on to the front of the Eld's throat, while his fingers curled around the back of the Amsir's neck. From there, he figured, he could start setting himself up a little more comfortably around here. He didn't know exactly what the Amsirs could really do to get him something to eat, for instance, but there was a whole world here, full of brave, strong, big-mouthed, edible people, who were used to doing what the Eld told them. And if the Eld had to do what Jackson told him . . .

But the Eld had had the thought to hobble Jackson's ankles with a loose leather strap while he slept, and Jackson fell down.

The Eld grinned. 'In a few days, it won't be necessary to do that, or anything like it. Then you'll be waking up with only one thought. If need be, I may remind you that breakfast is inside the Object. Then you'll turn to with a will.'

Lying there, thinking all kinds of top-of-the-head, fast-answer thoughts, Jackson said: 'I believe a lot more in you for breakfast than in any guesses about what's inside that thing.'

The Eld said: 'It's truly amazing what you may believe in a few days. It's not a pretty condition. I think you'd disgust yourself. I don't think you would like that any more than I would. We have let you sleep. Here's some water,' he said, setting out one of those sealed hide bubbles of theirs. 'That we can give you. We won't be shocked – I won't be shocked – if you smear some on your skin. Does your arm hurt?'

'Thanks.'

The Amsir nodded off over Jackson's shoulder, and the doctor came up again. He unwrapped the bandages while Jackson drank and stared off at the rim of the world through the legs of the houses. When the doctor was done putting fresh wrappings on the arm, and was restoppering his bottle of liquid he said: 'Your arm's not healing. You'll lose it.'

'I knew that yesterday,' Jackson said. He tossed the water bubble down. 'There's something you can work on me with,' he said to the Eld. 'Maybe there is something in the Object that can fix my arm. Some kind of real doctor. Why not? If there's a feast for me in there, there might as well be healing, too.'

The Eld was untying the end of the thongs between Jackson's ankles; his wings got in his way a little, and he was clumsy about it, but he got them off anyhow. There were a couple of spearmen standing around, Jackson noticed now. It hadn't mattered before if they were there or not, because when you make that kind of play there's no point counting odds. But he had shot that one, and he noticed them now. He held still.

'And if not healing, why not anything else, too?' the Eld was saying as he worked. 'Indeed, why not? Why not females, why not any other pleasures that might appeal to you? Why not weapons? And you've thought of weapons in there, haven't you?' The Eld looked up shrewdly, his eyes twinkling. 'Oh, haven't you!'

The Eld shrugged too. 'And why not? Why not? If you crack open a mystery from the beginning of time, why not have it contain all lore, all rewards for the shrewd and the odd? Then you can look down on us from the doorway every morning and poke fun. Pfu! Let me show you the answer to that.' He gestured with a wing tip, and a couple of spearmen hustled something forward from behind the Thorn.

The creature smiled winningly at Jackson. It smiled at the spearmen, it smiled at the Amsir Eld, at the instructor, and in fact at everything. Jackson had never seen anything so easily pleased.

It was a shame it didn't look all that pleasant. It stood just about his size, and it walked – at a guess – like a man. But it was a little hard to tell, because it sagged so much. It was like dough, and the colour of dough. There was no part of it whose skin did not hang down in sloughy folds, except at the very top of its head, where little fleshy pseudopods spangled half-erect, about where an Amsir's crest of lace would have begun. The rest of its flesh hung on its frame of bones and meat, half-closed its eyes, drooped around little beginnings of ears, made a flabby ruff round the neck, hung in a brief, scalloped cape around its chest and upper arms, made another fold below its waist, and fell on down its legs. It was, if it was dough, some Amsir housewife's too-watery bit of kneading from which an Amsir pastry might have been baked.

All this delighted it. Its soft flap-fingered hands – the little finger rather longer than the others – twiddled constantly at its thighs, its shoulders, and its face. It seemed to love playing with its forefingers, quite frequently.

The Amsir Eld looked crookedly towards Jackson. Jackson obliged: 'All right – what is it?'

'Oh, this is Ahmuls,' he said. 'He's of a kind of creature born to us now and then. He happens to be one of the few who does not die while still very young. Well, his mother was a foolish woman and fond of him. And I'm very grateful to her now. You'll see why. Ahmuls is very lovable,' the Eld said as the creature shuffled up to him still twiddling. The Eld reached out and lightly stroked Ahmuls's cheek. 'Good morning, Ahmuls. I love you.'

'Good morning. I love you,' Ahmuls said rather clearly. He hummed some sort of contented sound and stroked the Eld's cheek.

'Ahmuls – this is Jackson,' the Eld said, pointing.

'Jackson . . .' Ahmuls said reflectively, opening his eyes with thumbs and forefingers as he focused his attention.

'Ahmuls, I want you to show Jackson something.'

'Oh, yes.'

'Very good,' the Eld said, stroking Ahmuls's face again. 'Ahmuls, hit that for me.' The Eld pointed to the leg of a house a dozen dozen running strides distant. The Eld threw in an aside to Jackson: 'Like many odd ones, Ahmuls has had to be special, or go under. He's very proud of things he's taught himself to do. They show he loves himself, and since we all love ourselves so very much, when we do something for that sort of love we're superb. Ahmuls . . . ?' The Eld looked questioningly at Ahmuls.

Ahmuls turned to one of the spearmen, floppy-fleshed arm extended. He said neither please nor I love you. The Eldish sudden uplift of his arm did all the necessary asking for him. The spearman didn't seem offended. He gave his javelin a bit of a toss and Ahmuls caught it in mid-air, thumb down, with his arm crossed in front of him, still turned three-quarters away from his target. The next Jackson saw of him clearly he was already stepping forward, his muscles already relaxing again, and the javelin was going through the air in an absolutely straight line, whirring. Jackson had never seen anything thrown that didn't curve down towards the end of its path. A dozen dozen running strides away the head of the javelin went into the house-leg with a *klat!*, a whip of its metal body, then a crack as the shaft snapped away from the immovably dug-in head. Up above, indignant voices boiled out, and heads and bodies showed at the doorway. Then a voice came faintly down, pleased as well as scandalized: 'Oh, Ahmuls!' And Jackson had been shown what love could do.

The Eld said: 'I love Ahmuls,' and Ahmuls grinned and grinned.

Pfu! thought Jackson.

The Eld stepped forward and took gentle hold of Ahmuls's arm. 'Watch, Jackson.' He pulled the flesh tight, for just a moment, and there was the outline of the human arm trapped under the uncooked-Amsir skin.

'You see,' the Eld went on to Jackson, 'this is also why I love Ahmuls. But let me show you that, too. Ahmuls – climb the ladder. Show Jackson you can climb the ladder, Ahmuls.'

Ahmuls held his eyes open again, hunted, found the two things he had to know about. 'Jackson,' he discovered. 'Ladder.' Satisfied, he was beside the Object with two strides, halfway up the ladder with one jump, and at its head immediately thereafter.

He stood with his feet curled over the top rung, and the only thing that kept him from falling backwards was that he leaned forward with his arms outstretched, oozed tight against the curving surface. While the door growled, he rubbed his face against the metal and moved his flattened palms in little caressing motions. Jackson raised an ear with a twist of his neck that reminded him about his arm, and could hear Ahmuls very faintly: 'I love you.'

'Come down now, Ahmuls,' the Eld cried. 'So you see,'

he said to Jackson, 'the door thinks Ahmuls is your kind of creature, for it doesn't kill him. True, Ahmuls is very stupid, and so there's no hope of his ever opening the door. But that's good for you when you think of it, for if Ahmuls weren't stupid, I wouldn't need you. Anyway, Ahmuls goes in with you, if you open the door. He knows enough to hit you if you pick up a weapon. He's been told all about it many times in the past. He will understand something if it's said to him a few times. He's too gluey inside to forget it after that.'

Ahmuls had come back to the Eld. They exchanged touches again. 'Love you,' both of them said.

Jackson studied them.

The Eld said to Jackson: 'There's only one way you can keep Ahmuls from waiting just below you on the ladder while you try the door, and then following you in. That would be to cripple him now. I still need you, and I have no replacement for Ahmuls. You wouldn't be punished, and you'd have a much better chance once you got inside. So I'm perfectly willing to let you try your luck right now.'

Jackson shook his head at the Eld and walked over to Ahmuls. He looked straight into Ahmuls's slitty eyes as he fondled the spongy thing's cheek. 'I love you.'

But Ahmuls wasn't having any. He caught Jackson's hand with something that felt like a five-fingered machine inside a cloak of blanketing. Somewhere inside all there, Ahmuls's sense of touch got a message through to his head. 'No good,' he said, rubbing Jackson's hand before throwing the arm aside. 'Soft.'

Chapter Nine

I

It was hot up at the top of the ladder with Ahmuls humming happily a few rungs below him. Jackson ran his hands over the door again, and again found that it was exactly like any other door, except that it didn't have a handle, and it talked. He had got used to the growling. There were those scratches around the edges, where various hands before him had tried to pry. One or two of the scratches actually went maybe a fingernail-thickness deeper than the surface. The Eld had told him they were places where everybody sooner or later came to scratching in old scratches, trying to just plain wear through. The Eld's best estimate was that the deepest scratch had taken about a dozen men, working day and night, for maybe two weeks a piece. And it was as thick as a fingernail. The doors in the Thorn were as thick as two arms. But it was possible, Jackson thought, that a week or ten days from now he might start telling himself maybe this door wasn't that thick – maybe it was only a finger thick. Probably, the last two or three days he could hang on up there, he'd be telling himself he'd wear through any minute now.

The door was easy to get mad at. It was just another oval seam in the metal. A sensible man with other things to do would tell himself inside of an hour that it wasn't a door – it was some kind of fake wrinkle in the metal. He could climb back down the ladder, and never try again. There wasn't even any place for the voice to come out. It was the first time Jackson had ever met anything that could talk but didn't have a mouth.

He put his ear up to the door, trying to hear the heartbeat he could feel through his fingertips, but when he did that the voice went through his head, and he couldn't hear anything but it. He leaned out as far as he dared, and looked it up and down again, and then he said: 'Hey, Ahmuls, let's go down.'

'Down?'

'Down. Let's go down.'

'You're stupid,' Ahmuls said, but he moved obligingly down, one rung at a time, making sure Jackson came with him. The instructing Amsir, who'd been keeping a sharp eye on this public tooling, came hurrying up to them. 'What's wrong?

Ahmuls grinned and pointed at Jackson. 'He came down. He's stupid.'

'I've learned all I'm going to, up there,' Jackson said.

'Where else are you going to learn anything?'

'That's the real problem, I guess – answering that one. But I've learned everything I'm going to, up there,' Jackson said, and walked towards the Thorn.

'Don't you leave me!' Ahmuls cried, taking Jackson's good arm.

'It's all right, Ahmuls dear,' the instructing Amsir said hastily. 'You wait here – I'll bring him back. He'll be with me.'

'All right. But you bring him back,' Ahmuls said dubiously.

'What are you going to do?' the instructing Amsir said, rustling along beside Jackson, his eyes glittering with intense curiosity.

'Study doors,' Jackson said. He jerked his thumb towards the Thorn. 'Quite a few of them in there.'

He stood in doorways all that afternoon, bracing his feet and elbows inside the oval door jambs as best he could, trying to understand how it felt to be that thick, that tall, that flat. He growled grudgingly out of various Amsirs' way whenever they came shuffling and scraping up the halls through him. He swung himself flat against a wall and stood that way for a long time, his fingers and toes curved around the jamb, being hinges. By the end of the afternoon, he had a pretty good idea inside his head of how a door would think and act and feel about people. But, always, only a door that had a handle through its middle.

By evening, the little hollow place that he dreamed through his middle, where the handle's works would be, had grown into something that he had to admit resembled the faint beginning of hunger in a man who let himself think about food. That was the only gain he had to show for the day, and he had to admit it was a loss. Towards evening, Ahmuls came looking for him, unhappy because the instructor didn't love him or he would have brought Jackson back, unhappy because Jackson still wouldn't go back up the ladder, unhappy because the sun was going down and it was time to go back, to sleep, to wait for morning and the ladder, and Jackson again, and meanwhile not be loved.

II

In the morning, Jackson climbed back up the ladder. Ahmuls patted him approvingly on the shoulder as he stood aside to let him by. 'Now you're smart,' he said.

'Glad to hear it,' Jackson said. The doctor had re-done his arm again, with the usual results. Jackson could feel that arm all the way up his neck and into the inside of his head this fine morning in the bright sunlight with all the happy Amsirs flopping in the sky above him, and Ahmuls slurring and slapping up the ladder below him. When he got to the top, he sat down facing outwards, leaning his back and the back of his head against the metal, his feet resting on the next rung down, letting himself warm up. He kept his arms crossed over his up-bent thighs.

He began to talk casually. 'You know, door, I spent a long time last night trying to be like you.'

The door said: 'Ouwwtenshownnn. Dhayss dwuuhrr uhhpnnss owwnnuhhli . . .' and so forth.

'Didn't do any good. Man can't be a door. Can pretend to be a door – can tell himself he is a door. But a man doesn't have hinges. Anyway he doesn't have the kind of hinges a door does. And a man can't be a door like you at all, because a man has handles.'

'. . . dhaysstroydd wiyethouyut dhaysscriyeshunn,' the door said.

'Then I got to thinking to myself, door,' Jackson said, paying no mind as the door began again.

'Hey! You talkin' to me?' Ahmuls said peevishly from below.

'No.'

'Awwll ouwwthrr uhluff-ffouwrrmms . . .' said the door.

'I got to thinking that if a man can't be a door, can a door be a man? And I guess we both know the answer to that. You're stupid, door. You tell the difference between my kind of creature and a Amsir; you're supposed to keep Amsirs out, so it figures maybe you're supposed to let men in. I mean, even the instructor has got that much figured out. And their Eld has it figured out, so that clinches it. But you won't let me in. You don't knock me off, but you don't let me in. You don't knock Ahmuls off either, and that's a mistake. No, no two ways about it – you're stupid. So I got to thinking, how do I make myself as stupid as a stupid door that thinks it's a man.'

'. . . wieyethouyut dhaysscriyeshunn.'

Jackson turned his head in a way that looked pretty casual and idle, and would have been casual in somebody whose arm didn't hurt all the way into his head. Ahmuls was right there, looking up at him. Over the many times Ahmuls had had this kind of duty, he'd learned that if he hung his head back and twisted his shoulders so that he was looking upside-down, he didn't have to hold the loose skin away from his eyes. 'Love you,' Jackson said.

'You're awful,' Ahmuls answered decisively.

'Well, I was saying, door – you're stupid. But you've got ears, and you can feel, and I guess you can see, too, even if you can't talk straight.'

'. . . t umm-nn pehrrsowwnnuhll.'

'Now the thing is, door, if you won't let me in, and you won't let Amsirs in, what did you ever let out that you *would* let back in? It would have to be something that talks like you, but looks like me, wouldn't it, door? Or, anyway,' Jackson said, listening to Ahmuls hum through the sound of the door going on talking, 'anyway something soft. But you've been here since the beginning of time. What happened to what you let out, way back then? Door, I figure somewhere you've got a picture of what you should let back in. A picture that talks, I guess, but I figure that's what you've got to have. Something to let you compare. Something you're too stupid to forget.'

It was getting hot again. Jackson wiped his face.

The instructing Amsir was getting all excited down below. He cupped his beak in his hand and shouted up: 'Ahmuls! What's he doing up there?'

'Nothing.'

'Then why has the door stopped growling?'

Jackson took a long, deep breath. He turned around and looked at the door, holding it tight with his good hand and with the best he could do with his bad one. It would be no time to fall off now. 'You dumb door!' he said. 'This is only the first thing I thought of to try.'

Down below him, Ahmuls was shifting his grip too, forgetting he couldn't see as well right side up as he could upside down.

'All right, door – if I've got you started thinking again after all this time – all right, if you do listen better than you talk, then you figure out what you let out would look like by now, and you figure out what it would talk like. It can't be that hard!' he said, suddenly irritated. 'If that instructor can figure out some of your words, then something smart enough to tell the difference between a Amsir and a man should be able to figure out my words. *Open up, you dumb bastard!*' he cried.

The beat of the Object's heart changed. There was a creak, a suck, a pop. The door jumped back the thickness of a finger, and zipped sideways, into a place made for it to slide into the skin of the Object.

Jackson scrambled around on the ladder. Down below him the Eld was a little slow getting things organized. There were spearmen throwing from down there, but they hadn't really got themselves set.

The whole thing was happening too fast for everybody. Jackson hadn't really figured the door would make sense out of what he said, and for all of his talking, the Eld hadn't figured Jackson would get the door open this fast, if ever. So that buggered up all the Eld's quiet, unspoken thinking about how once the door was open he didn't need Jackson at all, because he had Ahmuls or could maybe get other creatures of Jackson's kind who maybe wouldn't be as tricky. Well, all that thinking was shot, too, because Jackson was in through the door, and into a dark little room banging himself up, laughing and cursing, before the spearmen got into the air. In fact, the only one who stayed cool was Ahmuls. He'd been told what to do a lot of times, and now he did it. He came flipping in through the doorway, and stood next to where Jackson was lying on the floor. 'I come, too,' he said, happy to be useful.

Jackson let out his breath as the first couple of spears came buzzing in through the doorway from nervous, fluttering spearmen. He ducked as they clattered off the walls. 'I guess you do.'

There was this other door at the end of the little room. There was a red, bright lamp shining over it. Then the outside door closed, the light went out, yellow light came on from overhead in the little room, and the inside door opened . . . *thuk, wink, wink, thum*! Past it were all kinds of things that looked like what Jackson guessed was Thorn-like machinery. Through the metal around them, he and Ahmuls both could hear the outside door hollering as spears hit it. Its voice was too fast, too high. It sounded as panicky as everybody.

'Attention! Attention! This system has now been adjusted to accelerated speech mode. This door opens only to human personnel. All other life-forms will be destroyed without discretion. An intelligible warning has been given.'

'It was about time,' Jackson said.

Chapter Ten

I

'What's happening?' Ahmuls said unhappily, peering into the inside of the Object. He'd jerk back his head to look over his shoulder every time another spear point hit the other side of the door, but then he'd peer again. Things were beginning to hum inside the Object. Jackson could see light getting brighter, dancing around in there; he could hear things going clickety-click. Most of all he could feel how strong the Object was becoming. All around them, a frantic voice like the voice of the door said: 'Uhhcumminng uhup t full pow'r!' Farther inside the Object the same voice cried: 'Standing by on full power! Main generators On, maintenance power supply Off!' The voice steadied down. It began to sound as if it felt normal. You could even tell it was a woman. 'Condition of vessel report: All systems functional and reliable. Maintenance Mode battery drain excessive; recharging.'

'What's happening?' Ahmuls cried.

'Don't look at me, chum,' Jackson said quickly, 'I haven't picked up any weapons.'

'You better not!'

'I know.' Jackson had his feet firmly under him and moved to the doorway that led deeper inside the Object. 'Will you look at all that machinery!'

'What are we going to do! Who'd want to stay in here!' Ahmuls wailed.

Jackson listened to the *tang! tang! tang!* of spears hitting the outside of the Object. 'Oh, I don't know,' he said.

'Is anyone going to take command?' the door-voice said.

What? What now? Jackson thought. Any minute now, this clown was going to decide something was a weapon, and now there was this. Wasn't anybody in charge?

There was all this humming and buzzing; these voices talking and doors opening; all these things happening that he maybe could have enjoyed, if he'd come on them a little bit at a time, ready to take them on or take them apart. Maybe be them, or maybe picture them. But with a stomach and an arm and spear sounds and a Ahmuls like he had, he didn't feel all that ready.

'Command must be exercised within a reasonable period of time,' the voice said.

'Huh?' Ahmuls said.

'Command *must* be exercised! Stasis wastes power!'

Nag, nag, nag, Jackson thought. Whatever stasis is. 'All right,' he yelled. 'What'll make you happy?'

'Function. Duties to perform. I cannot come to full power for nothing!'

'Listen, you quit talking to it!' Ahmuls said. 'You done enough already.'

'Listen, no weapons, right?' Jackson said to him, holding out his empty hands. 'I'm *supposed* to talk to it, remember?' He raised his voice. 'You got a name, voice?'

Ahmuls was frowning, Jackson guessed. Maybe he'd stay busy that way just a little bit longer.

'My name is Self-Sustaining Interplanetary Exploration Module,' the voice said. 'Call me Susiem.'

'What can you do?'

'Anything! Anything a Susiem can do.'

You wouldn't think that was a lot of help, Jackson thought. But there was one thing he knew a Susiem could do, and it was with doors. He jumped, and bounced off Ahmuls. Ahmuls fell back. Jackson fell through the doorway farther into the object. 'Close that door!' he yelled. He lay there on the floor. He found that to the now more distant, and less frequent, sound of spears against the outside, was added the soft *klop!* of Ahmuls, trapped in the little room, beating his fist against the door.

Jackson shook his head and looked around. The room he was in was full of machinery; metal and glass all over the place, humped, twisted, full of knobs and pointers, flashing and gleaming, humming –

'That's great. But I don't see anything to eat.'

'Certainly not! Do you think you're in the mess compartment?' Susiem said.

'You trying to say there's another room here? Where there's food? There's really food?'

'I can do anything a Susiem can do!' Susiem said.

Klop, klop, klop.

'Boy, he talks plainer than you do,' Jackson said. 'All right, how do I get to that other room? And don't open that door until I say so! By the way, if you've got food, you wouldn't happen to have a doctor?' Jackson grinned. After that I want a Thorn where everybody wants to be like me, and Amsirs that want to give up to me. What you got here, Susiem – so much to give, a man could run out of dreaming? Not in the life of creatures of my kind. Well, come on – come on – work up a doctor for me. Give him gallons of boiling water, and a pile of clean rags big enough to sleep in.

'Certainly I won't open the door! You're in command! Report to Sick Bay immediately.'

'They got food there?'

'Medical treatment takes precedence over rations. Report to Sick Bay.'

I'm in command, Jackson thought. 'Where's Sick Bay?'

II

Susiem led him to Sick Bay by simply having him follow lights. They kept turning on just ahead of him as he walked through a door and then down a ladder and through another door. Sick Bay was all white except where it was bare metal. The doctor was white and bare metal, and had wheels. He unstoppered himself from a doctor-shaped hole in the wall and came rolling forward like a plough. He came to about the height of Jackson's chest. 'State your complaint,' he said.

'My arm's going to have to come off,' Jackson said, looking at the doctor carefully, deciding to believe Susiem when she said 'This is a doctor.'

'You're not competent to prognose. State your complaint. How do you account for the fact that you don't match any comparison in my files? Show proof you're entitled to receive medical treatment from this station.'

'Emergency, Doctor,' Susiem said. 'This man is in command.'

'You'll have to fill out forms,' the doctor said. A hard, soft-white square on its top turned a very pale white-green. A stick popped up most of the way out of a hole beside the square. 'Take the pen.' Jackson pulled it out curiously. It was the same shape and about the same length as the burnt sticks he had left behind at his home Thorn. But it wasn't burnt – it was light, felt soft at the surface but was as rigid as metal, felt slick, but didn't slip from his fingers. At the very end of it was what looked like a little ball of glass.

'Well?'

Jackson peered at the green-white square. There were lines running across it now, bright white. At the beginnings of the lines there were shapes of some kind – patterns made out of lines, bent and crossing each other. 'Kind of pretty,' he said.

'Criticism is not your function. Fill out the forms.'

'I think he's illiterate, Doctor,' Susiem said.

'Well, let him make some kind of mark,' the doctor said impatiently. 'I'm sure there are others waiting. He's wasting time.'

'He's in command.'

'Well, then he certainly ought to be literate.'

'Look – I order you to make yourself understandable,' Jackson told the doctor. 'My arm hurts, and I'm hungry.'

'Do you know how to make a mark? Make a mark on the surface of the plate with the light-pen. I have to have some sort of identification for you or I can't file you. And if I can't file you, you're lost.'

'Oh. You just want to be able to find me again. Well, here's what I look like.' The little ball slipped much too easily over the top of the plate, if that was what you called it, but the light-pen, or whatever, left a nice white line behind it. Jackson started turning his wrist to thicken and thin it, and that didn't work, but by and large he had a pretty good picture of himself down on the plate very soon. For good measure, he took one corner of the plate and made a drawing of his arm bones, showing where the dart had gone in. 'That's what's wrong with me. The dart's been pulled out, but the arm died.'

The doctor and Susiem didn't say anything for a little bit. Finally the doctor said: 'Your knowledge of anatomy isn't bad.'

'Draws well, too,' Susiem said. 'You can tell what you're looking at. Not like the paraphrastic stuff they do.'

'The arm,' Jackson said.

'Certainly the arm,' the doctor answered. 'Uh – Let's just have an overall look at you while we're about it.' The doctor shimmied back and forth on his wheels for a moment. There was a little humming plough-noise inside him. 'Hmm. Yes. Well – you've certainly led an active life. But it's all healed very nicely – barring some of the fresh events, of course. The only one that we need to do anything much about is in that elbow joint. You're going to need a restoration there. Your blood sugar is a little low. Are you fatigued?'

'Huh?'

'Are you tired?'

'Damn right. Hungry, too.'

'Well, I can introduce a little protein into your system, I suppose, while we're working on the arm, but I'd rather you had something to chew and swallow. It sets up a good reflex series. Susiem, why don't you get the Captain here some nourishment while I'm taking care of this.'

The doctor came apart, partway, with some kind of flip of his sides, which turned into a kind of chair-cradle. The seat and back, and part that went under the legs, were padded, and so was the place for Jackson's right arm to rest. A trough that extended partway into the doctor was for Jackson's left arm. It was bare metal, and a little bar of light popped out on a stalk over it, lighting up the leather wrappings as Jackson sat down.

'Sick Call takes precedence over Mess,' Susiem said. 'I see no reason why he can't be treated and then go to where the food is.'

'I said bring him something!' the doctor snapped. 'He's undernourished, he's got one arm free to serve himself with, and besides, rank has its privileges.'

'If you record it as a prescription, Doctor.'

'I do.'

'Very well,' Susiem said. Something began to stir around one compartment lower down. 'I'm breaking out a food cart.'

'For a machine,' Jackson said to the doctor, 'you got more sense than people.'

'Damn right,' the doctor said. 'Now let's get this slop off your limb. Who's been treating you – some veterinarian?'

'Some what?'

'Captain, you need an education.'

'What's that?'

'What you need.' Maybe the doctor didn't want to go around and around any more; maybe he figured he could keep Jackson busy with something else. At any rate, something that must have been a knife zipped down the length of Jackson's arm. It laid open the wrappings as neat as any slash Jackson had ever seen. It laid open his arm too, and it sure did cut down on his desire to do much talking. He sat there staring at his own bones, pink-white, in the halved shell of his arm. All around the torn, discoloured place where Red Filson's dart had gone down in on its way to the elbow joint, it looked like something rotten.

Sparks – maybe metal, maybe light – winked and flashed around the bone. There was a cloudy white puff of fog where the joint was; there was a suck of air and that was gone, *whummph!* and then the joint was gone. The bones of his upper and lower arm didn't meet by a full third of a dozen finger-widths. More sparks, and now the ends were notched and drilled, the way a stick-maker might make a pegged splice. The rotten place in the meat of his arm was getting smaller. His whole arm was tingling. The bar of light above it seemed to be shivering.

Something like a little doctor came rolling in the door, and flipped open its top. Steaming warmth hit Jackson in the nose like the clout of a damp, hot rag. He'd never smelled anything so strong in his life. It poured right up his nose and seemed to fill his whole head. He blinked; it was making his eyes water.

Lying on a dish were some greens with something greasy-looking on them, a round ball of something white and made out of small parts that looked like maggots, and a rounded squishy-looking brown thing that looked like what you might find under a Amsir house, if it had been dried. Next to it was something with a long slim handle and four long curved points, a folded-up white hunk of something that might have been Amsir lace shaved until it was thin and crinkly, and a glass of what would have looked like milk if it hadn't been so white and opaque.

'Lunch,' Susiem said. 'Salisbury steak, with Roquefort salad, and rice. Enjoy it, Captain.' Jackson couldn't make up his mind whether to look at his lunch or his arm.

The doctor was really getting things done in there. Delicate stilty little fingers with hinges in them came popping out, from under the same overhang that the bar of light came from. They were carrying a woven white contraption that looked like an outline drawing of an elbow joint. The little fingers put pegs in place, and in a trice where his broken elbow had been was this white thing, snugly slipped into place. He could see right through its weave, of course, but it looked pretty strong and solid all by itself.

'Okay,' the doctor said. 'That's what we call a jig-splint. In a couple of days, you'll have a pretty good structure of bone cells forming around that grid, and in a week or so that'll be as good as new.'

The two halves of Jackson's arm were pushed back together as the walls of the trough gently squeezed shut around them. The trough wiggled its halves back and forth for an instant until the halves of the arm were lined up just right. Then they fell back and where the cut had been there was a very thin line, like the scratch of a playful woman, running along the seam. For the first time, Jackson saw blood. It stood up in droplets like pinheads along the scratch, already scabbed and hard. The cut lengths of arm wrapping lay in the trough for an instant and then puffed out with a flash, a fog of smoke, and a *whoomph!* 'Eat your lunch,' the doctor said.

Jackson tested his arm. The lunch still looked like what it had looked like before. The arm was great. He twisted and stretched it, making a fist, squeezing, trying to see if it would pop open into two halves again. It wouldn't. It was a good, well-made arm. He rapped his left elbow with the knuckles of his right hand. It sounded good and hard.

Chapter Eleven

I

It didn't seem possible he had eaten. But Susiem had said: 'If you think I'm going to throw away this perfectly good food, and go to the trouble of synthesizing burnt Amsir and whole grain bread, when the whole basis of your being here is that you're *human* . . .'

Jackson had to admit that Salisbury steak, rice and Roquefort salad wasn't bad. He licked the leftovers off his fingers. But he drew the line at what Susiem called milk; he finally got some water instead.

He sat back. The doctor was still letting him sit in him. 'You know,' Jackson said, 'it's funny how it works out.' Here the Eld Amsir had been jollying him along with lots of fine talk about maybe there was food in here, and something to do about his arm, and be damned if there wasn't. Who could tell that, and send the luck to him? Where was there a place from which the luck-sender could have that kind of vantage? Was there Ariwol after all? Believe in luck, believe in Ariwol, huh? Rather not believe in luck. What do you call it when it comes, then?

'What are your further orders, Captain?' Susiem said impatiently.

'Well . . . I don't know. Is there some place around here for me to sleep?'

'You don't need any right now,' the doctor said.

'*Sleep!*' Susiem said simultaneously. 'Here you've got everything turned on, and you're going to *sleep*?'

'Well, it's something us humans do. Whether they need it or not. Can't tell when your next chance is going to be.'

'Humans,' the doctor said, 'sleep at set, regular times.'

'That's right,' Susiem said. 'Stasis wastes *power*!'

Oh boy, it never stops, Jackson thought, even with machines. 'Well, look – you must have had other captains – '

'I should say so!'

'What did you do when they slept?'

'When they slept, the First Officer was awake. Don't you know anything about being human?'

'He needs an education,' the doctor said.

'More than I need a First Officer?' Jackson said.

'What about the individual in the airlock? Isn't that your First Officer?'

'Him?' All Ahmuls was in Jackson's head right now was a *klop, klop, klop* on the inside door. That was enough. He still hadn't decided what to do about that. But why did he have to decide now? It wasn't as if he was going to spend the rest of his life anywhere else but here. Being Captain . . . whenever the machines didn't have something else in mind. 'What's a First Officer do? I got one's pretty good with a spear, I guess. But spearing don't seem to be much needed. I mean, you're made out of metal, Doctor, and I don't even know where you are, Susiem.'

Susiem giggled.

'All right, that does it,' the doctor said. 'I'm prescribing this boy a university. You do have the necessary fact library, don't you?'

'Self-Sustaining Interplanetary Exploration Modules are, self-evidently, self-sustaining,' Susiem answered, as the doctor's arm immediately, but gently, unfolded additional sections that held Jackson by the wrists. The seat changed slope, so that he was mostly lying down.

'No need to get offended about it. Just be ready to patch through into my inputs when I say the word. And no stirring around in *my* banks while we're overlapping, either – everybody thinks all *they* need to be doctors themselves is facts. Get the leukocytes and the cytoplasms in their right places and anyone can be a sawbones! That's what *you* think. So stay out and do your job, and I'll do mine.'

What the hell were they up to? Jackson made one try at getting his arms out, which taught him he couldn't do it. Anyhow, supposing he'd get loose, where was he going to run to? Outside? Through the little room with Ahmuls *klopp*ing in it? But what the hell were they up to? Round pads came from somewhere behind Jackson's head and pressed it close among them, front and back, both sides.

'All right, I'm hitting him with the predisposants now.' A little thing like a hollow spearpoint whipped out of the doctor's insides, darted at Jackson's throat, stopped short but close, and fired something cold and stinging into the place where the heavy throb of blood came near the surface of the skin. Jackson felt it just for a heartbeat, and he was still admiring how fast it moved and how keen it looked, when it flipped back and disappeared. 'Massive dose,' the doctor commented. 'With this individual, you want the same dose as you'd need to teach a horse symphonic composition.' Jackson could feel something very funny happening to his eyes and ears. Sounds were beginning to break up into little reverberating pieces. First the edges of everything he could see were blurred, and then he was weak. Moisture – great glittering streams of tears – pooled out of his helpless lids and sheeted down his face.

A bulky, warm feeling spread out from the pit of his stomach. His fingers felt as if his palms were split painlessly and smoothly along each string of bones clear back to the whites. The same time his eyes ran wet, his lips were puffy and dry, and the same time his belly was warm, his forehead was icy cold. He swallowed, and his ears popped. He blinked, and his tear-filled eyes felt sandy. 'He's ready,' the doctor said.

There was another fine, cold spray at the back of Jackson's neck. 'Inputs going in now.' Something fine and ticklish as Petra Jovans's hair came in through the back of Jackson's neck, slipped gracefully to the inside of his head, and for all he knew quivered there. 'All right, patch in,' the doctor said.

Whatever patching-in was, Jackson guessed Susiem had done it, because suddenly, inside his head, where he was, there was a feeling like – A thing happening like – Well, what was happening, was that, in there, and around there, what was being done – no; what was happening –

'Who could I tell?' Jackson hollered at the top of his lungs. 'Who would believe me!'

11

It was no different, really, than remembering what it was like being a boy around the Thorn. One day he was just another brat – just another brat, except he was inside himself – and the next day he was here in the expeditionary ship, remembering it. It was probably no different from that.

'Well?' the doctor said.

'He's done,' Susiem said.

The taste of hot dust was in his mouth, swirling up around the Thorn as he ran, and ran. The feel of the first time he swung his arm just right and the dart shot straight and true into the target, a buzzing streak of what Honor White Jackson could do. Honor Secon Black Jackson. Honor Red Jackson. Honor Red Jackson, hurting and hungry, being a door in the alien echoes of the Amsir Thorn. And now he was here. Memory had no time or space.

His head was very full.

Hey! he thought, I was right all along! It was too small – it was all too small, and it was all wrong. I was right and they were wrong.

When he thought of how they tried to keep him down, and how they kept themselves down, he began to grin. When he thought about the Amsirs, poking and prying, trying to understand it all – from where they were – he grinned even more fiercely. Oh, wow – mine is the Earth and everything that's in it.

'Congratulations, Captain,' Susiem said, 'you are now an Honours graduate in Liberal Arts form Ohio State University. You have a special Master's in Command Psychology from the University of Chicago, and three semester hours in military journalism from the Air Force Academy. You are fully qualified to command this vessel.'

'I know that,' Jackson said.

'These qualifications are now on file in my data banks, and will be listed with Earth Central Statistics immediately upon my reacquisition of contact with the Associated Midwestern

University Generic Research Project communications network,' Susiem went on, tidying up the loose ends.

Jackson had loose ends of his own. He barely heard her. What he heard, through the fabric of the ship, very softly but very much on his mind, was *klop, klop, klop.*

'There's no way you can tease him out of that airlock and back down the ladder, is there?' he said, *pro forma,* but he didn't want to do that anyway. Poor bloody Ahmuls. If he got him out of the lock and back to the Eld Amsir's love, what use would they have for him with the ship gone? And the ship would be gone. He most certainly wasn't going to spend his life grounded aboard her now, even supposing her life support system could endure that long with his organism draining it. But that was secondary, too – in fact, irrelevant. For who, knowing him as he was now, knowing how much time there was to make up for, could imagine him going anywhere but Earthward?

Earthward to Ariwol, he noted parenthetically. Earthward to Airworld. The tongue of his mind twisted voluptuously around the ability to make the long vowels flow; he took a deep, deep breath – breath enough to make him giddy.

Klop klop klop.

Kick him out, struggling, to ridicule and scorn, to uselessness with the ship gone? How could he do that to a creature at his mercy that he did not ever need to eat?

Eat.

'What about this lichen they eat? Can you synthesize that for . . . our shipmate?'

'I can do anything a Susiem can do.'

'It's a perfectly normal Terrestrial form,' the doctor said.

'Oh. Then there's no problem. Let's bring him in. We'll control him long enough for you and Susiem to do as much as you can for his brain and data file, and it's solved.'

'It is not. You're already proving a little learning is a dangerous thing. In the first place, I don't know what you mean by control, but I certainly wouldn't take on any hostile organisms of his size with one limb as fragile as that arm of yours is at present. And you don't seem to have drawn the proper conclusions from his diet. I am amazed you were able to survive out there at all. I have no predisposants that could possibly do anything useful to *his* nucleic acids. You're anthropomorphizing. To all intents and purposes, there is less kinship between him and the human heritage than there is between you and me.'

'That's ridiculous!' Susiem cried. 'He's perfectly human – he can't fly, can he?'

'If you don't want your mistakes brought up, ship, don't activate doctors.'

'All right, you two, cut it out,' Jackson said. What the hell did the doctor mean, he couldn't control Ahmuls? It was perfectly plain how he could control Ahmuls – he'd been told about it in his sophomore year. What he hadn't been told was how to like it. But he'd also been taught how to get along without liking, while going for his Master's. It was amazing the things he'd been taught. 'Doctor – all right, you can't predispose him. Can you patch him up if he's hurt?'

'No problem,' the medico replied.

'Susiem, if we let him in, can you protect your components in that room?'

'To an extent.'

'Well, then, let's get to it – I'm sick of this place. The sooner we get this done, the quicker we can move.' I wonder how he'll like Ariwol.

He walked up the companionway to the airlock level. He put his face up close to the door. 'Ahmuls! Ahmuls, can you hear me?'

'You son of a bitch.'

'Listen to me – if I open this door, what'll you do?'

'Kill you, you son of a bitch.'

'Ahmuls, listen close. You may not believe this, but I can bust you up real good.'

'Not if I kill you, you son of a bitch.'

'Ahmuls, I'm telling you – they gave me a – ' What had they given him? They'd given him a weapon, and he had picked it up.

By the time Susiem and the Extraterrestrial Life-Adaptability Technique Experiment were launched, the art of unarmed combat on Earth had reached a point of development which made practice unnecessary and the karate-ka's calluses superfluous. The system had been refined to so simple a point that a mere explanation of what places were to be touched was sufficient. Any man with a decent memory for instructions, and reasonable dexterity, could successfully apply it to an equally proficient man with slower reflexes – and to all uninitiates – with cunning rapidity and shocking accomplishment. Jackson's reflexes were not as quick as Ahmuls's but his memory was as fast as Susiem's feed to his brain, and in any case Ahmuls just had no idea –

'Aw, hell,' Jackson said. 'Susiem, open the door.'

It was amazing how fast the sport was, bags of loose flesh and all, flapping and grunting, his feet slap-slapping, his pudgy hands extended from his forearms as if he wore ragged sleeves.

Jackson extended his body, right forefinger first, and touched him as he had been told in the fieldhouse amphitheatre of the sunny Canterbury Gothic campus. It was shocking how Ahmuls's feet flew out from under him. Jackson reached down quickly, and touched the one ankle he could reach: Ahmuls cried out. He probably hadn't often felt pain. Not since he'd got big enough.

Jackson moved back out of the way. 'Look, Ahmuls – you can't get up to catch me now. Will you listen?'

But Ahmuls could get up. People did walk on broken legs – they even ran on them, when they had to and were in shock. It was just a matter of how much actual physical incapacity was introduced into their physical structures. Until things really disintegrated, they could just keep running. It happened on football fields and in parachute-jump training all the time. The uneasy part about it was, it often made them run faster. That was how Ahmuls was now.

Jackson wove around Ahmuls's charge. His reflexes were slower, but the method was foolproof against charging attacks provided the eye could register them at all. He touched Ahmuls on the ribs. After that, Ahmuls's side was like a rawhide bag of blood. Goddamn it, don't smear on me! Jackson thought as he made Ahmuls brush by him again. Aw, you dumb animal! 'Give up!' he yelled.

Ahmuls charged him, grunting: 'Leave me alone – leave me alone, will you!'

Jackson touched both arms. He had to take the shock of Ahmuls hitting him, but he took it on Ahmuls's bad side, and anyway, Ahmuls then had no arms to hug him with. He moved them right, but they bent in too many places, and Jackson got out through them.

'Get the doctor up here!' Jackson yelled.

'Watch out for my components!' Susiem cried as Ahmuls blundered.

'The hell with you and all your components!' Jackson yelled as he touched Ahmuls low in the back, feeling the flesh turn to porridge as the shock travelled from where he touched, and then he touched again in the same place, just to make sure; this time he felt the same thing in his fingertip you feel when you're a kid and you nudge out a baby tooth. Ahmuls windmilled his floppy arms, but he had nothing to hold his legs up any more, and he went down, folding in the middle and folding at the broken ankle, putting out his broken arms to catch him, landing on his broken side, and then his face. He lay slumped on his knees, arms out, his face squashed flat against the deck, and only one red eye peering up at Jackson.

'All right, all right,' he wept. The tears found hidden channels in his folded cheek.

Jackson dropped to his knees on the deck beside him. 'I tried to tell ya,' he said.

'Yuh.' Ahmuls swung his neck as best he could, very fast, going for Jackson's wrist with his teeth. Jackson pushed his head down. 'Cut it out; please cut it out.'

'Yuh. Yuh, all right, all right, I've got nothing left.' His fingers crept towards Jackson's ankle, dragging his arm, and Jackson put his knee on them. The doctor came rolling up. He stood there.

'Well, goddamn it,' Jackson squalled, 'what are you waiting for?'

'I have no authorization.'

'All right – pursuant to the emergency veterinary provisions, I declare this creature is a valuable, harmless alien life form in distress. I order you to proceed with medical services as far as your knowledge and experience go!'

The doctor's sides unfolded. 'Yes, sir. No problem.'

Ahmuls had quit trying to move his fingers under Jackson's knee. Under his face, the deck was wet. 'What are you going to do – What are you going to do, all you soft things?'

'No, no, it's all right, Ahmuls,' Jackson said. His hand on Ahmuls's head was making smoothing motions up where a Amsir would have its lace. 'The doctor'll fix you. You've got to listen, Ahmuls. Why the hell can't you listen? I love you.'

'Did you have to hit me?'

The doctor gathered Ahmuls up in his arms. He was amazingly gentle. He lifted smoothly and tenderly, making Ahmuls comfortable in his arm. He was shockingly gentle.

A maintenance machine had already slipped from its wall recess. It was hovering around the three of them, jockeying to get to the deck where it was messed up.

'Just wait your turn, Susiem,' Jackson said angrily, facing the maintenance machine as if it had eyes and ears. 'You have no sense of decency, no sense at all.'

Chapter Twelve

I

'Get me an audiovisual picture of the outside,' he told Susiem, sitting in the piloting chair.

Susiem swung a scope towards him. The speakers filled with the sounds of the outside; the rustle of wings, the murmur of wind, the ping and crackle of large expanses of metal in the open weather. The Amsirs were flying patrol just past the door, beating back and forth, spears ready. There was a littering of broken spears on the ground below the airlock ladder. At the doorway of the Thorn, the Amsir Eld, and the instructing Amsir, and a crowd of more than six but less than twelve apprentices of some type were clustered there, in postures that were not essentially useful. He could hear them discoursing; he motioned impatiently towards the gain control and he could make out their words. They were disputatious and bereft.

'And I tell you we must accept the possibility that we are the interlopers here!' one of them was saying.

'Shut up! I can clearly recall a witnessed discourse in which it was impeccably postulated that if the Object destroyed our kind on touch, how much more terrible must be the fate of any creature it would permit to enter its maw!'

'Shut up yourself! I'll try conclusions with *you* any time!'

'Eld!' Jackson said, and the Object growled to the Amsirs at the doorway. 'Eld – stand clear!'

'What?' The hard beak was up. The bright, dark eyes were searching where the doorway was on top of the ladder.

'Eld, I have some facts for you.'

The communicator went dead abruptly. The screen was blank, the speakers were silent. 'You are not permitted to contaminate the experiment!' Susiem snapped. 'You are exceeding your authority and directly contravening expedition regulations. You are not permitted to communicate facts to the experimental subjects. All facts required by the experimental subjects are predetermined, programmed, and were long ago introduced to the system. Any repetition of this incident will result in your automatic and immediate dismissal from command. This incident will be logged. It will be transferred to the central comprehensive files on Earth at the earliest opportunity following reacquisition of contact with the Project's communications network. You are reprimanded and are permitted to resume communication only on the basis that you make no further attempt at contamination.'

The screen and the speakers came back to life. 'Stand clear,' Jackson shouted to the Eld. He counted thirty seconds on the fascia clock. 'Let's go, Susiem,' he said, and with a bang and a roar and a flash they all went, taking the world's hope with them, while broken Amsirs crashed about.

II

Earth was pastorally green, its hillocks crowned by elms, its infrequent, low buildings starkly white. Earth was green, fair, and heady with the wine of life, in a condition not often attained since the hills of Greece were first so limned by the deft pencillings of Walt Disney.

It hadn't seemed like such a particularly long trip. He had spent large parts of it in the piloting couch. At first he'd yearned at the stars in their great glowing panoplies, bemused to think that he finally understood what they were, toying in his mind with thoughts of immensity, with notions of how vast it all was, how marvellous its creation, how unfathomable its extent. Fantasy-grasps of macrocosm and microcosm haunted his understanding. All this great clockwork, this explosion and decay, these cycles and epicycles of infinitude, distended his capillaries with shivers of delight at how vast a table had been prepared before him. For a while he thought he understood the infinitely tiny complexities that hurtled around about themselves to form each millimicrocubit of immensity.

And Susiem did much to sustain this feeling for him. She groaned and whined, thumping and jolting within herself all around him; his couch trembled to her humming. Each start of ignition, each fit of clicking busyness seemed to reflect another spasm of gobbling at the miles between where he was and the nebulae on which his eyesight rested.

But a couple of days went by and it occurred to him that the nebulae weren't getting effectively closer. He had a clear intellectual understanding of how many miles per day were being clocked on Susiem's instruments. He got the idea that he ought to calculate how many days of whining, banging, and groaning from this tireless mechanism he'd have to endure before he got to the nearest nebula. It came to him that there was just so much of that a man could put up with.

Susiem could put up with it forever, of course. Only somebody like Susiem was liable to want to.

'How's the doctor coming along with Ahmuls?' he asked her, thinking a good way to put it was that he was lonely among a myriad of stars.

'I'll check . . . He's reporting good progress. Considerable healing has been accomplished and the patient is resting. His manner is subdued.'

'Yeah, well. He's had a lot happen to him.'

He had Susiem close the ablation shutters on the piloting windows again. And for a while he had her run tapes of Earth. He found that it was just as he remembered it – swarming with Man and his works, beautiful beyond belief, busy in its beauty, echoing with flashes of light and sound, ashake with motion, singing of power to the morning and the evening wind.

He created little moments of naïveté for himself. He looked at the rivers tumbling down out of the mountains and rowelling across the plains while saying to himself, I never knew there was that much water in the world; how green everything is, how full! He looked at the cities where the rivers forked, at the shipping complexes in the deltas where rivers and ocean mingled, and he cried out to himself *Thalassa! Thalassa!* He compared the flight of supersonic aircraft with the flappings of Amsirs and he pretended to see a portable rocket launcher in terms of a demigod's throwing stick. He craned his neck at the cloud-raking spires of the mighty cities. And he made the back of his mind wail: 'Alas, Thorn!'

Ah, horse apples, he said after very little of that, being a man with a Master's, and had Susiem turn it off.

What to do? Jackson had another meal – this time it was delicious, because he knew how to order. There was even wine. Wine was considerably better than beer. But it left him moody.

He had Susiem play him some music. He read from her library, sticking mainly to entertainment; westerns, mostly, at first. Susiem's library had a first-chapter précis index; by using it lackadaisically and carelessly, he tripped over the Big Little Book version of *John Carter of Mars* and from there his taste spiralled outwards. He had got as far as G-8's struggle against the Kaiser's land aircraft carrier when Susiem passed him the word that Ahmuls was ready to be talked to.

'You feeling all right?'

'He feels fine. All his structural damage is repaired and healed. It was a massive job, but what with all the things I know how to do – and three days' sleep – he's fine.'

Ahmuls was sitting propped halfway up in a Sick Bay bunk, leaning back into a corner. There were shadows across his face. But he had his hands up, framing his cheeks, and you could see light glinting on his open eyes.

'How do you feel about all that?' Jackson said.

'Feel rotten,' Ahmuls mumbled. Jackson had to stop and re-think before he could understand him – he mumbled so fast, and so many syllables of his speech had drifted loose from the cleanly Midwest that Jackson remembered from his schooling. 'That doctor machine says we're going someplace.' Ahmuls mumbled on, and Jackson deciphered it all right, improving with practice. 'Where to?'

'Yeah, well. That's what I'm here to explain. You all done trying to kill me?'

'Can't kill you, you son of a bitch.'

'Aw, come *on*, Ahmuls. I'm glad you all done trying to kill me, but I wish you wouldn't call me names. Look, it's not like it used to be, all our lives. It's all different.'

'I'm no different.'

'Well, I am!'

'You say.'

'Will you listen?'

'Gotta listen. You can kill me.'

Jackson sighed and gestured towards a chair-cubby. The chair came promptly out of the wall. He sat down on it with the feeling that he might be here a long time. 'All right. So listen. Where we were before was a place called Mars.'

'Amirs,' Ahmuls repeated studiously.

'Okay, now there were these two places where people lived. My place and yours.'

'One place, where Amsirs lived. You're not people. Maybe I'm not people. But I'm not as soft as you are.'

'There were these two places where people lived. Amsirs and humans. But they came from the same place. The reason Amsirs looked different from people is because somebody wanted to see if people could be changed.'

'Humans look different from Amsirs. Amsirs are people.'

And so on. Jackson spent the better part of the rest of the trip trying to explain genetics to Ahmuls. But Ahmuls had the idea he already knew as much as anybody could teach him. He sat on his bunk most of the time, eating little brick-shaped packets of lichen as they were issued to him by Susiem according to the doctor's menu, and every so often either he or Jackson had to stop to go to the head. But he listened because Jackson could kill him if he didn't. This seemed to be something Ahmuls had learned long before he had Jackson for a tutor.

Finally, Susiem told Jackson they were only hours away from docking at Columbus, Ohio, and that he had better start getting presentable.

'All right,' Jackson said. 'Ahmuls, you hear that? Now pretty soon you're going to get a chance to really see something. You're going to see more people and more machinery than either you or me ever had any idea of. You're going to see the place we all come from. Your folks, my folks, the Amsirs' folks. We all come from the same place. You're going to get to see people living in houses stacked up two hundred houses tall. You're going to get to see places that make the whole place that Amsirs live in look no bigger than the way one Amsir house looks compared to the whole bunch of them. You're going to see things zipping across the sky three, five hundred times quicker'n a Amsir can fly falling straight down.'

Ahmuls said: 'How many dozen is that?'

'Oh, dear God. All right. *Don't* learn. I'm trying to tell you you're going to see things that you won't know how to act about. You're going to have more chances to be happy than you've ever thought of.' Well, it seemed reasonable. Wide as the world was, and as complex as he knew it could be, there had to be something in it for the poor freak.

For the poor, dangerous freak. 'And there's going to be lots of chances for you to be stupid, and for you to get hurt. So I'm telling you one last time – you don't want to learn, all right, you don't have to learn. But, by God, at least know you're stupid. Don't go pushing into things. Watch and wait. Walk soft. Maybe after a while you'll realize I'm giving you the straight goods. Any time you're ready, you just let me know and I'll do my best to tell you the straight of it again.'

'I'm straight now,' Ahmuls said, twiddling the flesh that grew on his arms where his wings should have been.

III

Just before they hit atmosphere, Jackson came down to Sick Bay to be with Ahmuls, knowing how the noise and the changes of acceleration would upset him. Jackson was wearing his Captain's pale blue coverall with the Associated Universities shoulder patch.

'What you got on you?' Ahmuls asked.

'This is clothes,' Jackson said. 'I had Susiem make some for you, too. Here.' He passed over the specially-cut coveralls. 'You got to put these on too. It's like a blanket. It keeps the cold and the sun off you.'

'I ain't never seen you wear clothes before.'

'Well, I didn't. But I know better now.'

'I don't know any better.'

'Look, you want them all to think you're a freak?'

'What, all those soft people you said all look like you?'

'Come on, Ahmuls, put the clothes on.'

'You going to kill me if I don't put the clothes on? I ain't cold and there ain't no sun on me. Don't they know enough to go into all of those big, stacked-up houses when they have to?' He dropped the coveralls on the floor.

Jackson shook his head. 'All right, Ahmuls. All right.' He stretched out on another bunk. His skin was already chafed in a couple of places, and he was having a hard time getting used to the whole idea of being wrapped up all around the legs and crotch. But he was very badly embarrassed at the thought of stepping out in front of a spaceport full of people with a naked freak at his side. It was, when he stopped to think of it, the first time in his life that he'd ever been embarrassed at first hand.

It was the damnedest feeling. It occupied considerable of his attention while the ship was coming down in her final approach. Ahmuls whimpered and lurched around on the bunk all through the process. What's going to become of him? Jackson thought.

But Earth was pastorally green, its hillocks crowned by elms, its infrequent, low buildings stark white. 'This is the site of the Associated Universities docking facilities,' Susiem said as Jackson stared out through the open airlock hatch, like a kid who had just watched a dart hit a target broadside on and then bounce off. 'There have been social changes on Earth since my last communication from the Project. I have just been assured you will be brought up to date on these changes by another source. You and your companion are instructed to debark from this vessel immediately, since it is no longer classified habitable. Attention, all hands! Captain going ashore!'

'Goodbye, fellows,' the doctor said as Jackson and Ahmuls slipped down the ladder. 'Don't worry, Ahmuls – your menu's on file. I'm told all you have to do when you get hungry is say so out loud.'

'Always did,' Ahmuls said.

Jackson looked up Susiem's height. She was beginning to ring. He noticed a swarm of bright, dancing insects whirling around the very tip of her prow. They were bulleted in from over the top of the nearest hillock, in a stream that thickened rapidly, divided to pass around the trunks and through the branches of the elms, and clustered more and more passionately around the tip. The ringing sound increased in volume, and he saw that Susiem was blunted. Her prow was gone. As he watched, the tightly spiralling insects ate another shaving of metal from her plates, and then came round again, cutting off a little bit more with each pass, passing very quickly. It was like a Looneytoon of termites destroying Elmer Fudd's house.

Some of the insects broke away from Susiem, and darted down towards the ground. One nearby seemed to be performing a typical action; it had a little chunk of astronautics-grade steel in its mouth, and it was spinning like an auger. It bored down two or three feet into the ground, Jackson judged by its speed, then back out empty-jawed, and immediately streaked back to snip off more.

Larger bugs came down out of the sky, burrowed into the exposed 'tween-deck spaces and the component arrays behind the stripped-out plating. They buzzed away again, trailing some few components in their grappling appendages, casting off most of the others, which fell in a swathe beyond the diminishing Susiem with sharp thuds on the thick, clipped green grass and delicate wild flowers. Ground-moving insects and other metal creatures of that kind were waiting to pick them over, chop them up into chunks, plant some, gulp down others as if they had digestions.

'Hey!' Jackson yelled, trying to get through to Susiem

before there was no one left on Earth to tell him what was happening. But it was way too late for that. She and the doctor and the food-serving robot and the maintenance robot and everything about her – except for Jackson's coveralls – were dead and useless. Well, no, not useless. A lot of valuable minerals had just been put back into Earth's soil.

Ahmuls was looking around. 'I see some people coming,' he said. 'They ain't got no clothes on.'

Chapter Thirteen

I

He was very heavy in the limbs. He wasn't slumped like Ahmuls was, but he was very heavy in the limbs. And Ahmuls was right – they didn't have any clothes on.

They were a big bunch of men and women, just less than twenty of them altogether. The first one of them – a man, with clean limbs, much more gracefully and heavily muscled than anyone Jackson had ever actually seen – had lithely walked up into sight from a hidden hollow nearby. He had stood looking at Jackson and Ahmuls, ankle-deep in the grass, with sparkling silver glints swirling around his head and shoulders like a short-lived cowl of daytime stars. Then the little insects had flown away into the sky and been lost, and the man had motioned to whatever was down in the hollow behind him. The rest of the people had come up.

They were all grown-ups, and they moved with a confidence that reminded him of Amsirs. They had apparently been doing something together down there out of sight.

Jackson felt heavy and he felt in layers, like there were two transparent picture screens laid over each other between him and them.

Looking at them, he knew what they were. They were people who had eaten right all their lives; lived right, had the right kind of doctoring. They were people sprung from the kind of person he himself had been when he was at Ohio State.

From the kind of person he had been at Ohio State, he knew how to look at himself now. He was undersized, gangling, knobbily long of leg, hollow-stomached. His skin was like the leather of a horse that has at some past time broken through barbed wire. His eyes were pits, icy blue without a trace of melanin, their whites like smooth, wet bone. His hair was a short, raggedly-cut thatch of brittle straw. In his coveralls, he was a parody.

Their men were too big; their women were too smart. They came walking in towards him and Ahmuls as if none of them had ever stepped on a cockleburr.

Well, what was he going to do? He couldn't even let them see him rip off his coveralls and be himself. It would be too gauche.

'See? Told you – no clothes.'

'Right. My apologies, Ahmuls.'

'Your what?'

'I mean I'm sorry.'

The buzzing of the insects had stopped. Now he could hear the murmur of the wind through the pliant grass, and take time to feel the warmth of the wonderful sun on his face and hands. He could even remember strolling along the shade-dappled groves of State in the April weather, and the slumberous delight of baking for hours in the sun of Jackson Park Beach when he was at Chicago. I'm home, he thought, I'm home where I've never been, and I have to stake my claim upon it.

He began to feel the onset of voices, murmuring as the people spoke between themselves. He shook his head to clear it, feeling the knots growing in the muscles of his neck.

They had reached him. Some of them raised their hands in casual greetings, and smiled. They were all taller than he was. One of them said: 'Hello, there! Comp tells us you're from that genetic experiment on Mars. Both of you. Tell you the truth, Comp had never told us about the experiment before. There was a great range of new data when that space ship came down with you and prompted us to ask about it. Biggest thing in years. It's great. Welcome aboard.'

Their accent was a bit beyond Midwest. But it wasn't unintelligible. He could already feel himself sorting it out properly.

Comp would be Central Control; the thing that guided the insects, that determined the fate of spaceships, of specimens from the – abandoned? forgotten? – genetics experiment on Mars, of the landscape which no longer needed more than a minimum of serviceable features.

It had happened here some time after Susiem's expedition had left to begin the – human, superseded – experiment. They had got their services properly centralized under one comprehensive control, and here he was, among the people it serviced.

But I'm one of you, he thought. My body wasn't built among you, but my mind was. I have come back from the apes and the jungle; Simba is an ailuropod carnivore to me, and Ahmuls is a pachyderm. And how shall I speak to you that you may know me?

'I'm glad to meet you,' he said earnestly. 'This is Ahmuls, and I am – ' A wicked little relay closed in his mind. He had found a way to license himself. He grinned. 'I'm Jackson Greystoke.'

II

He had said the right thing. They were smiling, twinkle-eyed. There was a brunette girl looking a little bewildered, but a golden-skinned blonde was scandalizedly dispelling her ignorance – Jackson could see the sweetmeat lips quickly whispering 'Tarzan, stupe!' before the blonde's mouth turned towards him and became a ripe plum.

The first man – maybe a little older than the rest, but maybe not; it was hard to tell, as it should be – was saying: 'Wonderful! Well chosen. My name is – ah . . . Kringle. These are my sons: Dasher, Comet, and Cupid. My daughters, Dancer and Vixen. My other sons: Donder, Blitzen, and Prancer. I'll let these other people tell you who they are – I wouldn't presume to. At any rate, come on, let's all grab a bite, and we can talk.'

It was amazing, being with people who could pick up like that. 'Come on, Ahmuls,' Jackson said, feeling better and better, lofted on a cloud of names as other people made introductions for themselves – Cincinnatus, Columbus and Elyria – Perry, Clark, Lois and Jimmy – Fred and Ginger – Lucky, Chester, Sweet, Home and Wings (who was the brunette again, and was glanced at with disappointment by some of the others when she gave her name) – Batten, Barton, Durstine, and Osborne.

He found that he got them all straight, and kept them all straight. They all fitted. Even when Wings said, shamefacedly: 'I did it wrong. Call me Pall.'

'I'm hungry,' one of them said from the back of the group.

'We're ready,' Jackson smiled. 'And thank you for the invitation. Let's go,' he said to Ahmuls again.

'Don't want to eat with you,' Ahmuls said. 'Don't want to eat with these people.'

A voice spoke in Jackson's ear. He felt the tiniest flutter of air, and out of the corner of his eyes he caught a glimpse of something bright, metal, and hovering. 'This is Comp,' the voice said. 'He needn't worry. There'll be food of his kind, too.'

Ahmuls said: 'What did it say?'

'He said he loves you. Come on.'

Some of them were already beginning to walk away, back towards the hidden hollow. Jackson took a step to follow them, stopped, frowned at Ahmuls, turned his head back to watch them go, then looked back at Ahmuls. 'Come on!' He moved quickly, and it felt heavy.

Ahmuls's eyes darted to follow his hand. 'Don't.' He got himself into motion, one hand to the right side of his face, holding his eyelids so he could watch Jackson from the farthest corner.

The group of them walked over the grassy rise of ground. Durstine, the blonde, murmured, her perfume very near to Jackson: 'I wish *I'd* thought of clothes.' Jackson stopped looking at Ahmuls and grinned at her. She raised one eyebrow back, touched her glistening upper lip with the tip of her tongue, and laughed.

Jackson could see Kringle frown.

Chapter Fourteen

I

The breakfast things were set down waiting on the grass, arranged to look nice on a broad, cream-white cloth that had doubtless been woven on the spot by bees. The graceful dishes were earth-colours, softly glowing, delicately drawn into shapes that seemed to float, waiting for palms, fingers and lips. It occurred to Jackson they were fragile enough to appeal to insects as well as Man.

They disposed themselves in comfortable attitudes upon the grass, the people did, Jackson with them. He breakfasted on tamales, tidbits, Riesling and conversation, while Comp's bees brought Ahmuls lichen.

They made no dishes for Ahmuls. Either Comp felt his hands would break chunks from any utensils the bees might make, or Comp was disinclined to produce anything clumsy enough to be sturdy enough. Ahmuls ate grumpily, peering at them all.

Jackson's senses were pretty busy with the vivacious scent of women, with the sound of words arranged and sung, not grunted or cawed, and with a horizon of perfect blue, thornless. When he did watch Ahmuls, it was infrequently, and from the corners of his eyes.

'It's not really so much different from the way you now remember it, is it?' Kringle was saying urbanely. 'I imagine you have the picture. When Comp reached the serviceability threshold, certain gross externals were modified very nearly overnight, but the verities remain.

'We still have the same old services: food, clothing – or the control of factors which once made clothing necessary – and shelter.' He gazed around him at the prairie grass, raised his eyebrows apologetically, and smiled at Jackson.

'Well, in actual fact the distinction between clothing and shelter has disappeared; in essence, it was dependent on the distinction between genial and hostile environment, and when *that* was taken care of . . . But you see my point. It's really very much as it was. People are the same. We feel the same things you remember – remember from old Earth and remember from Mars, too, I'll venture. We have our joys and sorrows, our social interactions . . .'

Kringle glanced at Ahmuls, at Pall, at Jackson again: 'There are little difficulties and large, as always . . . distinctions between individuals . . . levels of accomplishment . . . we tend to think our lives have an even tenor, since the externals are so efficiently serviced. And of course we are well-mannered, since we each share with Comp and none of us regards any other one as a potential source or drain of commodities; we need not cozen one another, nor speak harshly. You follow? Ah, I see you do. But –' Kringle frowned at a tamale '– set us down on Mars and what a change you would see, I suspect! In short order, the physically weak, the slow of reflex would be eliminated, yes. But the rest; ah, the rest would *not*. The animal is tougher than all that, wouldn't you say? I imagine that in short order I would find myself at the head of a numerically smaller group. Granted that. But I think if we were to postulate a thing called a "toughness index" . . . *compris?* . . . the measure of a certain basic quality, which would wane in those insufficiently participant in it (as some people will always be), but would wax in the remainder – You see what I'm driving at? The "toughness index" of the numerical remainder of this little group, on Mars would total certainly not less, perhaps more, than it aggregates now for the larger number.' Kringle smiled encouragingly. 'That would be the crucial factor, would it not? The measure of humanity? One might say that so long as the index does not lessen, humanity does not lessen, no matter what humanity's number might be at the given moment.'

'Nice reasoning,' Durstine mumured, speaking from close beside Jackson. She reached forward to pluck another bite from the platter nearest Jackson's feet. She turned her head to look up at his face, her arched golden eyebrows rising in enquiry. At his nod, she lightly handed him the bit of cheese and took another for herself. She moved beautifully, bending, plucking, handing, sitting back again in one composed flow.

Jackson let the cheese soften against the roof of his mouth. He had to admit he was barely listening to what Kringle was saying. And it was probably just as well, he made out from as much of it as had registered. But, wow, he thought, what a luxury of just talking, along with eating like this. And not a blessed thing to worry about, not a damned thing to need going out and hunting up to pay for all of this.

'Even today,' Kringle was saying, 'we are in a sense the select winnowing of a larger but perhaps less sufficient number. Consider that a great deal of the procreative urge is actually a reflection of panic – not a tough quality – and of boredom – certainly a symptom of insufficiency. I would place the world's population at, oh, five per cent of the number for a thousand years ago. Is this a tragedy? Well, I say in reply to that, can number be impressive where index is invariant?'

Kringle bowed his head slightly, smiled graciously, and sipped his wine, his hands cupping the goblet symmetrically, the whole gesture a declaration of structure completed. 'So now you understand us.'

Well, maybe not this morning, but I will, Jackson thought. That's the great thing about it – there's all this time and all this world. The Riesling's very nice in the morning here.

All around him were the soft voices. Who cared what they said? He was in with them.

He began to chuckle, watching Ahmuls with lichen in his mouth, and bees darting at his face. Jackson thought, who would believe it? Where are the Amsirs, and where are all the people who believed in Ariwol?

And yet, in looking back, he couldn't honestly say that he'd ever told himself there was something better than Thorns. He'd only never stopped feeling there was something wrong. And he had never even tried to change them. All he'd had was the sense not to let them change him.

That was all it took. Now go back and try and explain it to Black. Or his mother. Sure it was simple. All you had to be was Jackson Greystoke, lost among the primates, with a Tudor manor waiting for him at home on a sceptred isle.

He began to laugh even louder as it occurred to him what an incredible, marvellous, wonderful thing he'd done. He was here by right. He was one of them.

Watching him laugh, they smiled. Little Pall held out a cup of wine, her large brown eyes twinkling again as they had no doubt always been intended to. 'It *is* nice, isn't it?' she said. 'It must feel good.'

It was beyond his wildest dreams. He sat on the grass with his knees drawn up, sipping wine and feeling the heavy familiar touch of Earth upon him.

II

'So we're agreed, then, aren't we?' Kringle was saying, leaning forward far enough so there was a three-fold wrinkling of his heavily-muscled stomach. It occurred to Jackson that Kringle might be just a little slow of foot – if it ever came to running. 'There is no essential difference between you and – for example – myself,' Kringle was going on. 'With some exposure to your environment, I – for example's sake, I – would resemble you physically. And there are no essential differences of capability.'

Durstine's fingertips had found the ridge of the beak scar through the light fabric over Jackson's shoulder. Kringle frowned fleetingly, even though for the most part he kept his eyes on Jackson's face.

'I don't know. Have to have it tried, wouldn't we?' Jackson said reasonably. He looked around at the other people. They were all politely chatting with each other, nibbling, munching. Yet, now that he looked at them again, it seemed they had a reflex of looking at him the moment he looked at them. The women were about half and half; some of them seemed to be ready to play it Durstine's way, or Pall's, and others weren't. But they were ready to play it some way, it occurred to Jackson. The men . . . well, it was a funny thing, but they seemed to know that about the women. They seemed to know without looking at the women, while looking over towards Jackson.

'Tried?' Kringle said. 'It's been tried, hasn't it? We still have a common ancestry, you know.'

'Well, sure, but so do the Amsirs. So does he.' Jackson nodded over to Ahmuls. He flexed his shoulder under Durstine's hand, and winked at Pall. Columbus, over in among the group, there – the one who'd been so anxious to get back to breakfast – saw the wink. He looked at Jackson, slowly and thoughtfully cracking his knuckles.

Ah, so, Jackson thought. Enmity in Eden. Well, listen man, I've been going without for a long time.

And underneath that he thought with a little touch of doom that soon enough the novelty would wear off him, and they'd all be competing for their women on an even basis. Maybe a little less than even, he reminded himself, heavy in the limbs. He winked at Columbus. But soon enough ain't now, he thought.

As he turned his head back towards Kringle, he saw that lots had been going on while his attention was elsewhere. Kringle was taking little cubes of cheese and flipping them off the ball of his thumb with his middle finger. He was paying no obvious attention to what he was doing . . . just toying idly with his food on a pleasant morning, very much at his ease, woolgathering. But he was flipping every one of those cubes at Ahmuls. They were bouncing off the sport's chest and thighs, rebounding soundlessly, and falling into the grass, where bees pounced on them and doubtless immediately turned them into plant nutriment. Jackson looked from Kringle to Ahmuls quizzically. He took another sip of wine. Now, what the hell was going to come of this? he thought.

Gradually Ahmuls noticed. 'Hey – hey, you!'

Kringle slowly turned his face upwards, and opened his eyes wider, so that now he could plainly be said to be looking at Ahmuls. 'Speaking to me?'

'You doin' that?'

'I beg your pardon? I think, if you spoke more slowly, perhaps, then . . .'

'He wants you to cut it out,' Jackson said.

'Does he?' Kringle said back over his shoulder. 'Ahmuls!

Is there something bothering you?'

'Yeah. Quit doin' that.'

Kringle held up his empty hands. 'I have stopped doing it. What's your problem?'

'Don't hit me with that shit.'

Kringle raised his eyebrows. He picked up another cube of cheese, and, daintily holding it between his fingers, nibbled at it. 'What are you calling me?'

Jackson leaned forward to Kringle, grinning a little. 'Listen, don't let me butt in on anything, but he could tear you apart and be juggling the pieces before your feet stopped moving.'

'Could he?' Kringle's eyebrow-raised eyes looked momentarily back at Jackson again.

One of the tiny silver bees detached itself from the swarm around Ahmuls, zipped over to Jackson, and said:

'This is a Comp. Pardon *my* butting in, but I think you forget your own education. These people share it, and more. Furthermore, they know all about what happened aboard that obsolete vehicle. All the information in Susiem's files was naturally transferred to me. Therefore, it was fully available to them, and Kringle is among those who absorbed it.'

'You can always ask Comp anything,' Durstine murmured in Jackson's ear. 'He'll tell you. If you want to know a lot, one of his extero . . .'

'Exteroaffectors,' Comp said.

'That's right, one of his exteroaffectors will give it to you by absorption.'

Kringle flipped another piece of cheese at Ahmuls. It hit the tip of his nose. Ahmuls stood up.

Kringle stood up. 'Is there anything I can do for you, beast?' he said softly. Jackson could see Kringle's fingers taking on the appropriate tucked-in stances.

Jackson stood up. 'Let's everybody take it easy,' he said.

'But that would be against the nature of the beast,' Kringle said. He was taking time out to lick his fingertips. Standing up, his mouth was inches higher off the ground than the top of Ahmuls's head. You could collapse a spine, touching the head downwards.

III

'Listen, Ahmuls, he can kill you,' Jackson said. 'Look how he's holding his hands. You remember what that does?'

Ahmuls peered intently. 'Are you all that smart?'

Kringle cast a languorous eye back at Jackson. 'I'm not certain it's nice to come entering into other's people's conversations.'

'Well, I'm not sure it's nice, either. But I don't think it's nice to flick poison at people until they get mad enough for you to kill them.'

'Either it's not poison or he's not people,' Durstine murmured.

'Well formulated, my dear. *Keep* thinking clearly,' Kringle said.

Ahmuls was searching from one of their faces to the next while Durstine scornfully arched her back at Kringle and fluffed her hair away from her neck, deliberately touching Jackson on the calf as he stood beside her. Kringle was looking at Durstine. Only the bees looked where they were going, but as one of them tried to pop another crumb of lichen into Ahmuls's mouth, he growled, and his hand flicked out. He caught the buzzing silvery nugget. Durstine gasped. 'He's so fast!' Ahmuls flicked it towards Kringle. The bee spatted hard against Kringle's shoulder, and he clapped his hand over the white-centred blotch of redness that bloomed in his skin instantly.

'Ai!' said Durstine.

There was a rustling in the grass behind Jackson; he turned his head to look. The breakfast people were up on their elbows and knees and feet; they had stopped reclining or talking. They had their heads up, alert; their eyes shone, and their parted mouths drooped at the corners.

Kringle was drawn up; there was just the faintest snaky ripple of the muscles up one calf and thigh as he shifted his weight, and a fine, regular jumping began under the skin just above his left elbow. He lifted his hand away from the bee-bruise, and looked at his fingers, but there was nothing on them, and the bee had flown away, of course.

'Jump me. Jump me, animal!' Kringle whispered. He got his arms and legs ready; his fingers were stiff and motionless, and the moisture glinted on his lower teeth.

'Hey, I bother you, you know it?' Ahmuls said to him. 'Like around the Thorn. Was always the little and beat-out ones that made jokes on me. Only beat-out one that didn't, he was boss of the whole thing. Whyn't you lay off me? Maybe you'll be boss.'

'Just touch me,' Kringle pleaded in a whisper. 'Just lay the least little bit of a hand on me . . . please.'

Oh my God, my God, Jackson thought, visualizing what would happen the instant Kringle had an excuse for uncoiling. Ahmuls, you poor dumb son of a bitch – I knew you never had a chance here. Why didn't you listen? Why couldn't you *learn*?

'I ain't gonna touch you,' Ahmuls said. 'You think I'm crazy? You just leave me alone, and I ain't gonna touch you.'

'Leave you alone? You won't leave me alone!' Kringle moaned.

'Then I'm gonna go away. I ain't crazy about you.' Ahmuls turned to go, rippling turgidly, and began to move off. Kringle stared at him in pop-eyed astonishment.

'Come back here!'

'Won't,' Ahmuls said over his shoulder.

Jackson couldn't believe it, either. Where was he going to go? There was nothing out there but grass and white Walt Disney houses, and exteroaffectors. 'Hey! Wait! Hold on!' Jackson said, standing up. 'Don't just go out there like that!'

Ahmuls turned his head, holding his face so he could look at Jackson clearly. 'What's it to you? I ain't bothering you. Never gonna bother anybody like you. You people want this place, you keep it. You people wanna push me around, uh-uhn. S'lots of room. You gonna get tired of pushin' 'fore I run out of room t'get pushed to. You think I'm nuts, gonna get myself all beat up again, arguin' with you people? You're crazy!'

Where was he ever going to find a place that was going to love him? Jackson took a couple of fast steps and caught up to him. He put his hand on a doughy shoulder. 'Oh, come on now – just wait,' he found himself pleading. 'Look, we just got here. You've got to give it a chance. You've got to give yourself a chance. I mean, these people are some good, some bad, I guess. That's not going to keep me from being happy here. You could – '

'I'm not like you. I'm not like them.'

Kringle was walking up towards them. The whole feeling of everything had changed. He was grinning cockily. The rest of the men in the breakfast group were smiling and sneering at Ahmuls.

'Stop trying to mollify him,' Kringle said. 'He wants no part of us. He knows when he's whipped. He's right about one thing. He's not like us.' His glance flickered just very briefly over Jackson. 'Or you.'

Say, thought Jackson with icy ferret swiftness, suppose it turns out I can't live with these people, and then it turns out I can't even find Ahmuls, if he gets lost out there some place?

'Look, will you just leave us alone and let me talk to him?' he snapped at Kringle.

'Well, I don't see any need for you to be provoked into losing your patience.' Kringle walked away, back to the breakfast group. He reached down, deliberately took a tidbit from Durstine's fingers, and began chewing it with his front teeth, very delicately, while standing in front of her in such a way that she would have to reach around him if she wanted more.

'Come on, Ahmuls,' Jackson said.

'Say . . . Man to man on the prairie's endless waste, the sinewy Jackson Greystoke and his monstrous adversary faced each other,' Chester remarked.

Durstine laughed. She chimed in, 'The battle of two superb physical machines trembled on the brink of being joined. Here in this peaceful glade that had seen no violence in a score of centuries, suddenly there was a reawakening of Earth's age-old heritage of struggle between brute strength and trained intelligence.'

Donder declaimed: 'A still hush settled over the land, as Nature herself seemed to draw breath in shuddering anticipation of the awful onslaught.'

'What? What are they talkin' about?' Ahmuls muttered. Jackson looked over his shoulder. Durstine, and some of the others and even Kringle were staring towards him and Ahmuls, very much laughing-eyed. Some of the others had got back to just plain eating, gracefully sipping and nibbling. All of them were lounging about.

Pall seemed a little interested, but people with large, moist eyes frequently seem emotional when in fact they are merely displaying a phenomenon of physiology.

'Never mind,' Jackson said to Ahmuls. 'You just go on and do what you want.'

Ahmuls said: 'Right.' He trudged up the slope of the hollow, was silhouetted massively against the pale horizon of late morning, and began to diminish from the legs up as he lumbered down the other side of the slope and out of Jackson's line of vision.

Swift, once more, the underground pit-pattering flow of the thought. 'Comp – you'll keep track of him?'

'Oh, I always know where everybody is, of course,' a bee said in his ear. 'Even if I couldn't predict where they'll be. But I think there's no problem, predicting *him*. He'll find the place.'

'What place?'

'Room to roam around in, yet ideally suited for permanent food facilities. Places to play, and things to play with. He'll be delighted. He'll flourish.'

'What place, Comp? No, all you'll do is give me a name I don't know. What kind of place?'

'Kind of a zoo.'

'A zoo.'

'*Azoo, azoo, azoo, zoo, zoo,*' Kringle hummed, breaking into a waltz with Durstine. Chester caught up Elyria. Cincinnatus gathered Pall into his arms.

Soon they were all spinning over the grass like courting herons, humming, smiling, faces flushed, eyes laughing back over their shoulders, only Durstine winking at Jackson, only Pall looking momentarily bewildered, and yet she, too, was humming, '*Azoo, azoo, azoo, zoo, zoo, azoo, azoo, ah-zoooo, ah, ah, ah, ah, zoo, zoo, zoo,*' etc.

Well now, what do you do? Jackson thought. Scream at them? Be a monkey while they waltz? And so what if they *are* lunatics? Aren't they kind of cute . . . like a motorized sculpture of seraphim made out of razor blades?

Ahmuls was quite a distance away already; the dancers had made their point, and were stopping, sinking back down on the grass. 'I don't suppose you could educate him,' Jackson said to the bee. 'All you have are the total resources of a planet.'

'Don't see the need,' Comp said. 'Can I make him happier? Can I make him human without stealing his essence from him? He has no history and no future. All his yearnings are self-contained.' Comp knew when a point was made. The bee flew from beside Jackson's ear.

They were still flushed and giggling in the breakfast group. They looked at Jackson curiously, and he looked at them.

'Has your faithful companion left you speechless, then, Masked Rider of the Plains?' Jimmy enquired. 'Got your balloon pricked?'

'The only person he was ever faithful to is back on Mars,' Jackson said tautly. 'Unless that person's been busted. He misjudged me, you know.'

'Oh, come and eat with us, Jackson,' Kringle said. 'If you wish.' He lounged back with his arm around Durstine. Durstine rolled her eyes sideways and pouted seductively at Jackson.

'Yes . . . come and join us. Don't be miffed.'

Pall giggled. 'Funny old thing, galumphing off that way. And you should have seen your face when we all started dancing, Jackson!'

'Yes . . . almost as if he'd never heard of civilized habits,' Chester said, 'or never knew how to communicate.'

Jackson could feel himself winding up. If these people thought Kringle was something when he was in that mood, they had something to learn. . . .

'Jackson communicates very well,' Durstine said.

'Yes,' Kringle said. 'I think, Chester, Jackson would surprise you in his own milieu.'

'I'd have to see that,' Jimmy said.

'Well, it's entirely possible *for* you to see it,' Kringle said reasonably. 'If Jackson's willing.'

'I wonder if he would be,' Chester said.

'Of *course* he would!' Pall cried.

Turning his face this way and that as they spoke was like running from tunnel to tunnel, all full of cross-ways and no clues.

'Of course you will,' Durstine said in his face, soft and warm, with a half-twist of her body that brought her mouth and breath poignantly near.

'Will what?'

'Fight!'

'Fight what?'

'Amsir.'

'Why?'

'For me!'

'Where?'

'Here!'

'How?'

'No problem,' Comp said.

Chapter Fifteen

I

'What?'

'I can arrange it all. I can make an Amsir for you – excuse me; a Amsir – and a throwing stick and a couple of darts. I have some very good footage of the Martian terrain from my orbiters up there.'

'Orbiters? You mean you've got your eyes on Mars?'

'Certainly. We're not talking now about accelerating something man-carrying out to that distance. Our space exploration's quite sophisticated these days, compared to what it was when the primary system component was humanoid. But what I'm saying is that I have plenty of stock background. You go ahead and hunt your Amsir. I'll run in proper background and lighting. And perfect dubbing of the terrain. I am sure we can get you one hell of an audience for it. Wait one – I'll ask around.'

'Great response,' Comp said to him a moment later. 'We have over four hundred thousand lookers-in; thirty-eight per cent of the potential audience.'

'I don't think I understand. Thirty-eight per cent of the audience for what?'

'The audience for your actuality, man. Look, the number of the audience and the number of the world population are theoretically congruent, right? In practice there are always some individuals asleep and some urgently occupied otherwise. So there's never been a hundred per cent audience for an actuality – the live version at any rate. The record is eighty-three per cent, or thereabouts, but that was for the competition between Melanie Altershot and Charles Dawn, and a very long time ago. Well, I queried the population for interest in a Amsir hon, and they're all waiting – thirty-eight per cent of them are waiting now, and a number of others have expressed serious interest in taking it on the delay. It hinges now on whether you're willing. But I think you should know there hasn't been a thirty-eight per cent audience in quite some time.'

'You know, we don't have all day,' Donder said.

'Well, I'd like to do it,' Jackson said. 'Right here, huh?' Besides the impatience in Donder's voice, he had also noticed Vixen and Batten. The two of them now had some kind of flying toy.

It was a pale, translucent lavender. It caracolled back and forth between them as they stood some distance apart from each other and flew it from hand to hand. The object seemed to be to make patterns, for the marvellous toy trailed a feathery lavender wake which hung in the air briefly and then disintegrated into dusty filaments.

They had begun this game while Comp was explaining actualities to Jackson, and Jackson was busy listening. One or two people in the group had stopped watching Jackson and had started watching the flight; from being a tight group around Jackson, these people had begun to spread towards Batten and Vixen, attenuating. 'Sure,' Jackson repeated. 'Provide me with the tools and a Amsir, and we'll get with it.'

'Good!' Durstine and Comp said simultaneously. Pall smiled. Jackson smiled back at her. 'I know what it is,' she said. 'You never realized you'd get a chance here to do something you must have enjoyed so much.'

'Pall, darling,' Old said, 'one of the reasons I want to watch this is because it's done in a place where people do things they don't enjoy.'

Pall put her fingers to her mouth. 'Oh, Jackson, I'm sorry,' she said.

II

In this world, Amsir bones were made by insects. They came whipping in over the tops of the soughing grass stems, in a swarm far smaller than the one that had devoted itself to Susiem, each carrying a little white speck. They buzzed, they grouped to some efficient shape, and in a trice there was the stick. The place that would serve as the handle was properly shaped as if by patient sanding; the hinge was neatly fitted, the nock for the dart's butt properly incised. Jackson picked it up and admired it.

'It's a lot like my own, Comp. Those are good scanners you've got.'

'How about the darts?'

The short, bluntly-tapered hafts had been produced the same way the throwing sticks had been. The head was done by burrowing exteroceptors, who came spilling up out of the ground, clustered at the head of each dart as bees held it in place, and withdrew leaving cooling, jaggedly-pointed silicate heads fused into the cups that had been made there to receive them – each, for all Jackson knew, already freighted with its dab of synthetic Amsir-hide glue. He picked them up and bounced them in his palm. He rolled them around with his fingers. 'Good,' he said. 'Good, fine.'

He walked up the slope of the hollow and looked around. The landscape rolled away from him, empty. There was no sign of Ahmuls, or of anyone else. But there were a great many receptor bees clustering in the air up there.

'Look to your left,' Comp said. 'I am starting your Amsir.'

About seventy-five yards away the exteroaffectors attacked the grass. They darted down to catch stems being hurled up to them by others on the ground. They seized them and pulled them up into position. They moved with great rapidity, dexterity, and economy – it was as if the grass had freed itself of compliance to the breeze and had decided to bend its own way. It bent in all directions towards a common centre as the exteroaffectors took it, but as it bent it hurried forward rootless, and when it reached the centre it fountained up, urged by splashes of buzzing silver, and there before Jackson's eyes they wove a Amsir's bones.

Toe and tarsal, leg and knee, thigh and hip, they wove him from the inside out; spine, collarbone, shoulder joints, arms, elbows, forearms, hands – he watched the little finger extend itself like the shooting of a magic shrub. Neck and skull matted themselves into structural compactness. Now, flesh;

fibrous strands wrested into place upon the green bones. In a moment, he was all hooked up together. Then they clad him; hide was fitted; bubbles swelled. Beak and talons, crest and wings; lace, fluttering . . . fluttering pale; as he stirred there, exteroaffectors burrowing nimbly between the fibres to give him life, he bleached.

An army of burrowers came running forward, and fused the glistening fragments of his javelin. They tossed it upwards; a low cast, but his wing rippled as his right hand swooped down to seize it, and hollow-eyed, he straightened to turn his head and look at Jackson.

'Comp, your name is miracle,' Jackson said.

'My name is Comp.'

Jackson opened down the Velcro of his coveralls and shrugged out of them. Immediately, exteroaffectors clustered around him. He winced as they plated his body everywhere with themselves. But the touch was gentle, and they were gone again in the blink of an eye. 'Sunburn lotion,' Comp explained.

'Oh. Yeah, makes sense.'

He looked around to see what the breakfast group had made of all this. But there were none of them near him. They were all down in the hollow, sitting or stretched out gracefully, each with an exteroaffector on each eye, at each ear, on each hand. A little string of them, like a girdle of small jewels, lay across each stomach just below the navel. Jackson looked over at the grass Amsir standing alert in the middle of his patch of stubble. Jackson bent down, picked up the throwing stick and the two darts. The coveralls were gone, dissipated.

'Ready any time you are, friend,' he called to the Amsir.

'Ready,' Comp said in his ear, and withdrew.

III

The Amsir waved its javelined hand to him. Jackson took a few quick steps; running on grass was different, but he remembered. Remembering it gave him Ohio feet, instead of

Thorn feet, but at least it gave him feet. He tried a few dry casts of the stick, slapped the spare dart up into his armpit, and was off.

He was playing it about the only way he could; as if he and the Amsir had each turned a shoulder of a dune at the same moment and had spotted each other at a distance. He ran away at an angle, down and across the slope of the land, picking up speed, ready to dive and roll straight downhill if the bird cast its javelin.

The Amsir was turning. A thousand or ten thousand extero-affectors shifted its weight, raised its arms, cocked its hips, raised its leg. It tipped forward, planted its leg, raised the other, and was running like the wind, lace streaming, wings unfurled. It ran down and across the slope of the land, diagonally away from him, cutting across his line of flight, putting him in a position where he'd have to throw in the direction opposite to the one he was running in.

Shit! Jackson thought. I forgot how smart they were. He looked back over his shoulder. The dark, wide, empty eyes were looking along a wing at him. Jackson got his legs out in front of him and set his feet. He was sliding to a stop. The Amsir grinned, spread its wings, and hung stock-still in the air, legs free of the ground. Its knees bent; one wing dropped, the other rose. It landed faced around on a dime, claws sunk in the tough grass, javelin poised. Its legs began to scissor. It came on like an ostrich, straight for Jackson, eating up distance between them, confident it could duck.

For Jackson to get up any momentum to reach it with a dart, he would have to run straight towards it, now. If he ran to either side it would have a clear shot. And the best he could do would be to try something sidearm. If he ran away from it, it would run him down.

Oh boy, Jackson thought. All right, let's try one on you. He took three steps forward, simultaneously loading the stick, and then with the fourth step he fired.

Jesus, there was nothing on the throw. It was straight enough, but there was no whip to it; it was like throwing straight up. Or throwing with a sick arm.

I'm made of gruel in this place! he thought. The dart

might reach the Amsir, but it was a fool if it bothered to break stride long enough to duck. The dart would never get through its hide, but would hang tangled in its lace. Even if the dart happened to stick into him a little, it would have no stopping power.

The dart reached the Amsir, who swayed clumsily to get out of its way. But he'd miscalculated. He ran right up on it. It took him in the chest, on the lower left, and it just seemed to keep going in past all reason. It went in up to the butt, with the sound of shocked fibres. The Amsir's legs went out from under him. He spread his wings for balance, dropping the javelin.

'The dart. Give him the other dart!' Comp said quickly in Jackson's ear.

'Right.' The Amsir was all spread out, and had no traction. Jackson fired the second one, and this time he had enough practice really to step into it. He could feel it all up and down his arm and across his back, clear down to the sole of his foot, like a rope of electricity. He threw that dart harder than he had ever thrown in his life, and to reward him it took off feeling about half as good as it should have. But it got to the grass Amsir all right; it went in below his right collar-bone and it came out the other side, carrying about two or three yards beyond him, tumbling, looping down and bouncing on the grass, a trail of torn grass floating out in the air behind it. The Amsir's right arm folded back as if the hinge locks had failed on a carrier-based aircraft. He ground-looped around the surface of his left wing and nose-dived heavily to the prairie. You could hear his neck pop.

'He's dead,' Jackson said.

Comp said, 'Listen.'

The sound was incomprehensible. It sounded like what you might hear if you ran as fast as you could, dragging a spear point-down through rough sand. 'What the hell is that?'

'That's applause, Jackson. That's the applause of thirty-eight per cent of the world's population – with the gain turned down, of course.'

Chapter Sixteen

I

Jackson walked over to the dead Amsir. It lay sprawled where he had dropped it, all broken, Jackson's first dart just peeping out of its chest. There was a rustling and a shaking; it slumped, its tissues separating. The little metal insects came out of its fibres, and each took its little bit of dead grass away. Others came popping up to join them. The Amsir's wings became insubstantial; its body flattened. Its skull uncurled, and quick as that the burrowing exteroaffectors were scurrying off with its components, a straw-and-metal wave, still roughly in the shape of a broken Amsir's silhouette, hurrying through the grass, back to the stubble patch, there to return its elements to the soil. A buzzing cluster chewed through the javelin and the darts; Jackson dropped the throwing stick into the midst of them, and they snapped it up.

The breakfast group came up over the crest from the hollow, their faces flushed, their eyes sparkling. Dancer broke into a sprint towards Jackson, and as soon as one of them had done it, the rest followed suit. They came springing up to him, laughing, delighted with him. Jackson was watching the stubble patch, where clear droplets of water were forming on the clipped stems.

Kringle threw his arm around Jackson's shoulders and hugged him. 'Terrific!' he said. 'Just great!'

'You were fine!' Durstine gasped. 'Unbelievable!'

'Wouldn't you like to see it?' Pall asked.

'Yes! He ought to see it,' Jimmy agreed, and the rest of them took that up, smiling and laughing, pressing some sort of feast upon him.

Comp said: 'Here – '

Exteroaffectors landed like butterflies at his ears and eyes. They touched his palms and his belly.

'All that's involved in my getting in phase with the appropriate sectors of your central nervous system,' Comp explained. 'Just relax. Many people prefer to sit or lie down, but it's not necessary.'

They were all around him. Jackson had never had that happen to him before; all of them were radiating at least ninety-eight point six degrees Fahrenheit. At that temperature, they were creating all kinds of ranges of evaporation at their bodily surfaces, and none of them were insulated, nor was he. All kinds of effluents were being volatilized in close proximity to his olfactory receptors and the thermesthetic components of his own system. He sank down to the grass, hugging his knees. They sank down with him, all around him, smiling encouragingly and watching him. He closed his eyes. 'That's right,' Comp said. 'Now – here we go . . .'

II

The desert faded in. First there was a long shot of the two craters and the two Thorns, from a high altitude. The edge of the planet curved, nearly undiffused, against star-filled space. Then his point of view transited into tighter and tighter focus on the human crater, until it was a tight shot of the desert at dawn, reddish-purple, rolled up into dunes, with the harsh light of morning upon it. The point of view pulled in even tighter, until all there was to see was a flat, featureless, uniformly granular, unmarked field of desert-colour. The point of view held for a beat; then a Amsir's white claw flashed down into the middle of it, thrust in running stride across the granules, scattering them, flashed up and forward, out of the frame and was gone leaving everything as before except for the pit of its print, whose sides began to crumble and flow. Light sparkled from one granule, and Jackson's attention followed it as it slid down the side of the footprint. It had not touched bottom yet when, with a *thump!-thump!*, human running feet crossed quickly from right to left, kicking the Amsir-print out of existence, leaving their own.

The point of view shifted up, and he caught a glimpse of a running, naked Honor, and then, ahead of him, the bobbing form of a Amsir.

There was a jump cut, and the Amsir was running straight towards the point of view, grinning straight ahead.

Another jump, and now it was Jackson running by himself; for the first time, Jackson could be sure it was him and not a piece of stock footage, for he could see the scar on his shoulder, and then the profile of the uncapped face. His lips were drawn back. His teeth were white and wet; the side of his face, squinting, then eyes snapping wide open – every pore and every delicate blond hair growing whitely at the tops of his cheekbones above his beard. The cut this time was to a medium down shot of the two of them. Jackson was running, his head turned to look back over his shoulder. There was a shot of his feet jamming to a halt in the sand, fighting for purchase.

Now, the Amsir, braking in mid-air, changing direction.

Now, Jackson's first shot. The dart slapped into place on the stick. There was a beautiful slow-motion study of the muscles working in time, taken from behind him, as he made the recovery from his stop and worked the cast of his stick. As his arm flowed upwards with the dart butted in its nock, poised, head sparkling, the motion began to speed, until, as the dart came into line with the Amsir and he snapped it free, the motion went into overspeed. The muscles of his right arm and of his stomach twanged with force as he shot the dart, which whipped through the air and sank into the Amsir's chest. It came in so fast that the bird didn't even begin to duck until after he'd been hit.

Now the Amsir hung for a split second, in mortal trouble, wide open. The point of view jumped around Jackson in a carousel; he could see every move of his feet and legs, every twist of his torso, the tight strain of his left hand as he whipped it down, the flow of his right arm. There was an extreme close-up of the second dart in the stick as it whipped back across and below the horizon, then whipped forward again, as if the dart were motionless and the world were tumbling. Then the world stopped and the dart flew. Then there was a medium long shot of the Amsir taking the second dart and breaking his wings – actually seen in extreme close-up, reflected in the dilated pupil and the bottomless iris of Jackson's left eye. The background music, which had built up and over the sound of Jackson's forced breath with a crescendo of wood-block slaps, cut off. Jump cut to the Amsir's head impacting on the sand, medium long shot over Jackson's shoulder. SOUND: Neck Breaks (hold long shot; dub extreme close sound).

There was a medium close-up, facing Jackson, of him standing there, the empty stick dangling in his hand, his shoulders slumped, wiping his face and taking a deep breath. The point of view pulled back and up; there was a long shot, still trucking back, of Jackson looking towards the Amsir lying all crumpled up on the terrain, dwindling as the shot pulled back far enough so that the planet's horizon came back into view again. The camera panned to the stars, towards the sun, became filled with hot white light, and then on an accent clack from the wood blocks, cut out.

III

They were all around him; he opened his eyes, and they were sitting there right on top of him, damn near, touching him, grinning, laughing, saying: 'Didn't we tell you! Great! Absolutely great!'

Kringle said: 'I had no idea of how it was. It's never really possible to reach an intellectual grasp of a totally alien environment. That's why actualities are so superbly fitted to the didactic purpose. It's all very well to be given a series of facts for the brain to digest, but when you want to convey the immediacy of a situation, you've got to hit 'em right in the guts. Only way to do it. And I don't mind telling you, I've been hit.'

Vixen said, breathlessly: 'I feel as if my entire life's been changed.' She was hanging on to his arms. Well, people never believed a thing until they touched it.

'Hey, Comp,' Jackson said, 'why didn't I understand that thing? Was that supposed to be a Amsir hon?'

'I don't – oh. Yes, I do. You're talking about the editing and the direction. I should have realized; yes, I imagine it does look quite different in the finished version from the way it feels to you while you're performing the action. But you have to realize that the way it feels to you is made up of experiences, whereas to them it's made up of appearances. It would be dull as ditch water if I were to simply present a running record of the action from a fixed point of view. No, in order to give these people the feeling of what it's really like, considerable skill must be exercised in arranging the patterns of action in a way that will be meaningful to them. And it is meaningful; look at them reacting!'

'Full of tricked-up dub-ins, and shots jumping around like a nut?'

'It's what they need in order to be able to feel it. Believe me, a great deal of skill and intuition went into that production, and none of the effects were selected lightly. You want to remember, Jackson, that all you had to do was react naturally; I'm the one who had to manage it from scratch.'

'I suppose that includes the dumb way I was able to kill that fake in the first place.'

'If you're referring now to the Amsir's dull reactions at the crucial moment, you want to bear in mind that your reflexes and capabilities aren't yet co-ordinated with the physical properties of this environment. We couldn't very well have the Amsir hon you to death, could we?' Comp chided him.

Jackson shook his head. They were milling around excitedly, listening to exteroaffectors, getting all worked up about something new.

'What are you telling them now, while you're talking to me?'

'Oh, there's been a world-wide reaction to the actuality. I'm running a great number of delays to individuals who've been clued in by the live audience. Your total's well over fifty per cent, at this point, and accelerating. You're getting great word-of-mouth on this piece.'

Pall took his hands. Her eyes were shining. 'Jackson, Jackson, I think it's great! Do you know what we're going to do?'

''Fraid not.' He said it pretty gently.

'*Everybody* wants to meet you! We're going to have an – oh, excuse me! – *a* honning party!'

Jackson turned to Kringle: 'You're going to have a what?'

Kringle's eyes were twinkling. 'Watch!' He waved his arm, and the babble of cross-exclamations that had burst out among the breakfast group fell away to a background murmur. 'What do you say? Shall we have a Thorn?'

'*Yes!*'

'Comp . . .' Kringle said.

Oh, the sweet, passionate smell of them!

A dozen buzzings trembled faintly all around the horizon. Jackson turned to look. There were shimmerings around the low white houses under the trees. The trees themselves were glinting, and then trees and houses had disappeared in a silver mist, and the air shivered with sound of flying. Jackson kept turning, watching. Kringle chuckled.

The grass quivered everywhere, as if someone hidden under a bed had reached up and begun to pull on the blanket.

'I'm going to have to move you for a few minutes,' Comp said. 'If you'll just step on board. . . .'

Durstine tugged on his hand. '*This* way.'

Not all of Comp's exteroaffectors in this area were devoting themselves to the trees and the white houses. While Jackson's back was turned, some of them had put together a webwork of metal, struts and stanchions curving and curlicueing every which way, with hammocks and canopies extended from it, tassels swaying enticingly, fountains splashing coloured liquids from pool to lower pool to lower pool, step by step, to the accompaniment of delicately chiming music. It all made a ball of insouciantly variform nooks and crannies-within-crannies, yet open enough within itself so that the breakfast group's numbers could call back and forth and laugh to each other as they clamoured about within it. Durstine tugged him inside, and the ball lifted away from the surface of the prairie, drifting off at one side as it gained altitude, until they were all perched a hundred yards up in the air, reclining, clambering, joking back and forth, whispering excitedly. A pleasant breeze swept through the structure. Spray from the fountains tickled Jackson occasionally. Pall's upturned face peeked out from between two curling metal leaves farther down inside the ball. She wrinkled her nose at him and waved.

Meanwhile, Comp was making a party Thorn.

The ball drifted languidly above roaring torrents of exteroaffectors. They swirled through the air, rushing in from all directions, converging. Where they met, some swirled into subsidiary pools, others roared upwards in flashing combers, with little flecks of a kind of spray flashing away from their tips as they delivered their freight and went flirting away for another load. The fabric of the ball thrummed to the cataract sound; parts of it – leaves and flowers – began to chime in counterpoint to the fountain music.

'Look! Look!' Durstine breathed, her upper arm across his shoulders from a little behind him, her forearm bent to lie down across his biceps. Her voice was in his ear.

IV

The exteroaffectors pulled away from the plain below. Only a conical, thick cluster of them, a hundred feet across, hung in the air above the plain, and then these unwound in a spiral from the bottom. As they unwound, Jackson could see that they were finishing the upper stretches of the Thorn. Down on the ground, in a gay, fluttering circle, pavilions, bountifully striped and decorated, circled around the Thorn between a turf running-track and beautiful fields delimited by clipped green hedgerows. He looked again, and the Thorn was done; straight, tall, shimmering, with flags in its antennas.

'It's gorgeous,' Jackson said.

The cloud sank down to the turf between the Thorn and the pavilion houses, and everyone ran off to drink from the fountains. The fountains were spotted around its base, where he remembered taps. Pall was bent, hair falling about her cheeks in two short, sculptured wings, sipping from her cupped wet hands, where he remembered Petra Jovans.

Chapter Seventeen

I

The Thorn was warm, and gently yielding when he touched it. He couldn't make up his mind what colour it was; in some places it was off-black, with wine-dark highlights. As he shifted his gaze, he could see places where it was green as a fly. He stood back, gawking like a tourist, his head going from side to side, admiring the way the flagged antennas raked against the pure blue sky, enthralled by the power these people commanded, stunned by the munificence of it all, cupping his elbows. He thought: Was it for this, Red, to make a model for this that you strove, laboured, loved, and died?

'Oh, it's going to be such a great time!' Pall exclaimed, running up wet-lipped. 'Just everyone will be watching the actuality of it!'

Jackson nodded. 'I believe it,' he said gravely. Then he smiled, looking at her. What the hell – I mean, he thought, if she *looked* like a kid, you'd watch how you'd talk to her, now wouldn't you? He felt a touch on his arm. But this Durstine, now . . .

'Would you like to see inside?' she was saying. 'Wouldn't you like to look around in there?' She put her thigh up against his hip.

''Scuse us, Pall,' Jackson said.

'Oh, that's all right!' Pall piped. 'I have to go change, anyhow, and I want it to be a surprise!' She ducked off towards one of the pavilions.

Durstine chuckled. 'I'll be changing, too. But we have a few minutes.'

He followed her into the Thorn through a wide, elaborate doorway. It was like slipping into a sea of jewel soup.

The Thorn was hollow inside, all the way to the top, but webbed across in a tangle of crystal filaments that spun themselves up, glittering in swaying curtains and loops to disappear in the soft shadows overhead. Through the translucent walls of the Thorn came light; from here, the walls of the Thorn burst with all colours; green and gold, red and violet, blue and rust. The colours swirled and swept about each other in a pattern different from the not-quite-random swirlings of the inner webwork, which in turn took what it pleased of them and threw it back to Jackson and Durstine in a shower of shifting pinpoints. He looked at her, and she was mottled with glory.

She laughed and tossed her head, then stood motionless, looking at him through the lashes at the corner of one eye. 'Welcome to Earth,' she said. 'I wanted you to see this.' She turned gracefully, on tiptoe, raising one arm in a gesture that swept around the interior of the Thorn. It was hard to tell whether she meant the Thorn, or herself, or both.

'I wanted you to see what we can do. I want you to know what's yours, so you can use it, and grow with it, and claim your birthright properly.'

'Just my birthright, or other things, too? Could I take something that belonged to Kringle, for instance?'

She laughed. 'Some men have a birthright to anything they can lay their hands on.'

'Then I wouldn't stand so close, if I were you.'

'But I am. And I know exactly where I'm standing at all times.' She laughed, gaily, secretively. Her hand flashed out. Her fingernails trailed down his upper arm lightly enough, but by the time they reached his elbow they left a mark, and her middle finger, turning, drew a drop of blood. She touched it to her lips, and kissed him quickly on the mouth. 'I'll see you here again, a little later. I'm going to change . . . You might not recognize me gowned, ordinarily. But you will this time. I promise. Because, you see, of all the people in this world, I understand you best. Remember that when others tempt you.' She walked away a few steps, and looked back over her shoulder briefly. 'Remember. When the others twist around you, and that little Pall opens those eyes wide. Remember I'm the only one.' She walked away, her motions precise and intense.

Jackson watched her, thinking.

11

People were beginning to come into the Thorn; bees were listening to them, and exteroaffectors were beginning to pelt about, making and bringing whatever they wanted. There began to be music. Kringle came in, drifted over to the other side of the tent, and sat down alone on the floor.

Jackson noticed that the people weren't especially dressed. Oh, Elyria wore hoops of fine-spun wire around her neck in a golden cascade, and Donder had on a pair of black horn-rimmed glasses with flat windowpane lenses. Lois had clad one arm in silvery chain mail to the shoulder, and so forth. But it was the light that decorated them. As they shifted back and forth, talking, gesticualting, beginning to warm up to the occasion, they gained and lost patterns that shifted over their skins.

They were not eating or drinking much. They were talking, mostly. In fact, some of them were sitting very still, eyes half closed, heads bent, as if completely lost in private worlds. Often enough, one or another of them would smile at him, raise a hand, and look pleased to see him here. But none of them were really getting into conversation with him. They were much more interested in whatever it was that went on in their heads while they waited for a party to start swinging.

It was Vixen who started the ball rolling. Standing a little off to one side, she'd been frowning and swaying her body just slightly. Jackson had been watching her curiously, while he stood around waiting to see what would happen when Durstine – and Pall, too – came in. He happened to be watching when she suddenly snapped her fingers and said delightedly: 'Got it!'

'What? What do you have?' Ginger asked, and as Vixen grinned, heads began to turn towards her.

Vixen took two or three steps forward, walking in a peculiar way. As she moved, she seemed to gain confidence; her movements became more pronounced and regular, and a little smile played around the corners of her mouth. She walked that way to the centre of the circle made by the Thorn's floor. She had everybody's attention, now, and the light began to change. A glow began to come over the crystalline draperies, and soft, golden light began to grow in a dome, starting at the Thorn's floor, and working its way up the interior walls, until they were all standing in a crystal-clear bath of it.

'Jackson! Jackson – look!'

Vixen came walking towards him, one hand on her hip, the other extended in a graceful arch over her head, palm flat, fingers up. She smiled at him and reached with the other hand, and lifted something imaginary from the top of her head. She bent slightly at the waist, holding out her hands. 'Water, Honor?'

The party burst into applause. Vixen smiled shyly, laughed a little, and retreated. Apparently, it had been intended to be some kind of pantomime. But that wasn't how you carried water; you cradled water in your arms.

'Well! That was a good beginning, wouldn't you say?' Kringle said, slapping him on the back. 'I'd say she really conveyed the idea, wouldn't you?' He peered a little more closely at Jackson's face. 'No? Well, perhaps there were certain minor crudities in her performance.' A little knot of Vixen's particular friends was clustering around her, congratulating her. 'But it was certainly good enough for a beginning,' Kringle said.

Donder stepped forward. He stood in the centre of the floor, and raised his hand negligently. A hush fell over the crowd. Donder took a breath and began to speak:

'Die.
Be born, be loud, be free, but
die. Those of us born
Thorn-children suck that in our milk.
We hate you, Thorn:
We belch your word at you.'

He bowed to Jackson, flushed, a sheen of sweat across his brow.

They started to applaud. Then one of them remembered something, and began to snap his fingers. The inside of the party Thorn crackled with the odd sound of it.

'How 'bout that, Jackson?' Donder called out to him. 'Sort of puts it all in a nutshell, doesn't it?'

Jackson asked Kringle: 'Does he mean, the way you feel about the Thorn? I mean, does he think you should feel that way about the thing that keeps you alive?'

A very slight frown appeared between Kringle's brows again. 'I think if you examine your internal processes, you might find he came somewhat closer than you might be ready to admit.' He raised his voice and called to Donder: 'Beautiful, son! Now, gang,' he called out to the assembled company, 'we all want to remember that our guest isn't completely familiar with our customs. But we all know he's going to catch on in no time.'

Comp said in Jackson's ear: 'Listen, they need the feedback of your approval, or the party's going to lose its impetus.'

'Oh,' Jackson said.

'Look! Here's Pall!' Clark pointed at the entrance.

She came in shyly, holding her hands folded in front of her. Hanging around her waist was a ragged white drape of fabric; scant, pure unblemished white, high on one hip and low on the other, the loose, torn threads of its hem brushing her mid-thigh. She came walking up to Jackson, looking at the ground. As she got closer to him, Jackson could see that there were grains of sand worked into her hair, and streaked smudges from it on her body. They had clearly-defined edges, and they weren't any darker at the knees; there weren't little rings of it in the skin around her wrists, and there wasn't a deeper smudge of it at the base of her neck, in the hollow where perspiration would have washed it in the course of the day.

But by now, Jackson had the idea.

'Welcome home, Honor,' she said submissively, and the Thorn seemed to fill with the sound of the group's approval – a great appreciative roar that was compounded of applause and outcries of admiration.

'Tremendous!' Kringle said.

'Look at her, Jackson!' he lowered his voice. 'My dear – was that truly an original thought of yours? That's marvellous. Marvellous. Jackson, you do see it, don't you? She's made a work of art of herself. This is doubly exciting. Our little Pall . . .'

Pall was blushing. 'Thank you so much, Kringle.' She didn't quite know what to do with her hands; obviously it was the first time in her life she'd ever got a compliment for her creativity. 'Actually,' she said, 'you see, I'm such a naïve person, really – oh, Kringle will tell you I'm not, but he's just being polite – I finally thought to myself: "Well, if you're going to be naïve, and there doesn't seem to be anything you can do about it, you might as well do something constructive with it, wouldn't you think? Why don't you . . ." So I did! That's really all there was to it. I just did, that's all. I said to myself, the thing to do is take what you have and use it!'

'I think you did fine,' Jackson said. 'I think the subtle touch of presenting yourself not only as a work of art, but as a work of art with a duality of meaning is an example of the vitality inherent in the natural response.' He smiled at her, and touched her lightly on the shoulder. The thorn broke into fresh applause. 'It's of course the hard underlying base of the subtle but primary implication that really makes it work,' he said, looking sincerely into her eyes as they sparkled with fulfilment. Suddenly those eyes brimmed over, and two perfect tears flowed down her cheeks.

'Thank you,' she breathed so softly that the nearest sound receptor had to dart in a little closer, and hover like a humming bird at her lips.

III

Pall was circulating among the people, being congratulated by everyone, not just her particular friends. She walked like a débutante.

Jackson stood rubbing his left elbow.

Perry had been working at something behind a bunch of other people. 'Hey, look what Perry's got!' they began to exclaim, crowding around, with other people crowding in behind them, peering over their shoulders.

'Hold on, now! Everybody'll get a chance to see it!' Perry growled in a gruff, good-natured way.

Exteroaffectors carried it out to the middle of the floor for him, and put it up on three graceful, thin metal legs. High above, a rope of light kindled itself among the higher traceries of crystal, and concentrated its beam upon the painting.

'Jackson! Come forward, Jackson!' Perry motioned urgently from beside the painting. 'I dedicate this to you.'

Oh, Jesus! But Jackson got himself moving, his legs sucking up through glue, and went to look at it.

It had been done in wide, sometimes apparently laboured, sometimes apparently glib strokes. It was full of all the wrong colours. What it showed was Jackson's Thorn, in the distance, with the pale sun behind it. Huddled at the base of the Thorn were square, nearly featureless blocks that you could tell were houses because here and there there was a light in a window. In the foreground of the painting, mostly in silhouette, with only a few details picked out by highlights, was a Amsir lying on the blind slope of a dune, his head raised just enough so he could watch the Thorn and the houses. And off to one side, watching the Amsir, was the figure of a Honor, also blocked out crudely. You could tell it was a Honor because it was wearing something on its head that looked like a cross between the German helmets of World War II and the Franco-Prussian War. It was intended to be a honning cap, Jackson supposed.

You couldn't really fault it for skill. The guy had obviously done work of this kind before. You could maybe criticize the composition, but you had to do it on professional grounds. You had to give him that much. But, Jesus Christ, Comp had the right facts on file; they were there to be dug out. All you had to do was look for them.

'What do you think of it?' Perry asked, through the rising

sound of applause as the other people crowded around. Then he said: 'Of course, you want to feel free to use any terms you want – you don't need to confine yourself to the technical terms of the graphic arts.' There was an understanding little smile playing around the corners of his mouth. 'After all, many of my other friends here would have to use layman's language, too.'

Jackson opened his mouth, then closed it. He could feel the tip of his tongue rubbing against the inner faces of the teeth on one side of his jaw.

'Go ahead,' Perry said.

'Comp,' Jackson said, 'I need an easel, a backing board, a sheet of charcoal paper, and some charcoal. Right away, now.'

Perry looked nonplussed. The crowd around them grew quiet. The exteroaffectors worked quickly.

Another beam of light focused down on the blank sheet at Jackson's easel. He held all but one of the sticks in his left hand, and bounced the other in his right for a minute as he stepped back and looked around at the people. He sucked at his front teeth once, sharply, and stepped in to his work. He touched the tip of the stick to the paper. He drew them a Amsir, fanatical and brave, with a dart rattling loose in the hole punched through one of its main bubbles, trying to get one hand up and bent around enough to hold its fingers over the hole. Meanwhile it marched a Honor dressed in human skin and sucking on an air bottle towards the rim of the world.

When it was done, it was done. He didn't know exactly how long it took. Nobody interrupted him. They shuffled around, nervously, and sometimes whispered, but he was able to pay them no mind.

Looking at it, he could see it was all right; he had it right. His left hand was black and empty. He dropped the last stick on the floor, at Perry's feet. 'That's what I think of your painting,' he said. 'Technically.'

There was a gasp from several of the people behind him. Perry frowned and stepped around to look at the drawing. He stood scratching his chin, cocking his head back and forth. 'I'm . . . afraid I don't understand. What are you trying to say with this?'

There was a rising murmur of assent around the two of them. 'Yes. What does that prove?'

'Better let me have a look,' Kringle said, pushing forward. He stood beside Perry; Jackson had to step back to give him room. 'Hmm – are you trying to equate charcoal with oils?' Kringle asked Jackson in an avuncular sort of way. 'It's very difficult to compare art in different media, you know. In fact,' he pointed out reasonably, 'it's very difficult to compare art. *N'est ce pas?*'

'What I don't understand,' Perry said, 'is why he felt he had to be so hostile about it. I see what he's done here, and it's another scene entirely. How could one arrive at a basis for comparison?'

Donder said: 'Well, I think it's a hell of a note, any way you look at it! I mean, here Perry dedicated it to him, at *his* party – we're all taking part, here, for him. What does he want to act like this for?'

Chapter Eighteen

I

Just to make sure, Jackson took one last look at the difference between Perry's piece of work and his drawing. Then he turned around and worked his way out of the crowd. Many of them were trying to push forward and look at the twin centres of attention anyhow. The others glanced at him uncomfortably. Some of them looked a little distasteful, and others looked as if they didn't quite know what to do, but none of them could understand what he was so worked up about. So he was able to get out from between them without coming into any kind of contact. He wiped the sweat off his face, and then, looking at his wet, charcoaled palm, he realized he'd probably messed up his face pretty good. He walked out through the entrance and stood looking out at the pavilions, whose sides were responding gaily to the breeze.

'Comp, I want a ship.'

'That's impossible. It would be disastrous. You know enough about experimental discipline to understand that. Look,' Comp said soothingly, 'you're in a mood of despair. But that's the result of your failure to relate properly to these people – '

'Or their failure to relate to me.'

'There's no need to become emotional about it. By the way, I don't think you're as accomplished an artist as you believe yourself to be. I think there's very little rational ground to choose from between yourself and the individual called Perry. Therefore your disgust with his effort is founded purely on your emotional conviction that you are the better spokesman for that certain representation of reality. You may be right, but one representation of reality is no more worthy than another. Perry could choose to represent some portion of the world personally experienced by him. If he did, your attempt to copy it, no matter how many actualities you had seen and no matter how empathetic you felt, would not be as valid as his. Would it therefore be totally invalid? No, and Perry would be rude to say so. He would be almost inexcusably rude to demonstrate the fact as dramatically as you chose to do. And then of course there's the ultimate sin, you failed to make your point conclusively.

'All these things are working against you at the moment. But really, these are all things from which it's possible to recover. I think in no time at all you will have found a way of expressing yourself that is satisfactory to both you and the community. Well, perhaps not in no time. But in finite time. Relax – knock around a little. Learn what suits you best. Meanwhile – here – ' Exteroaffectors settled on him momentarily, and were gone. He was clean again, fresh-minted. His skin glowed. He rubbed his elbow. Maybe someday he'd be all hollow inside?

'Maybe I could offer a course in Throwing Stick? How about art? I mean, I could do something, and then you could have an election and see if it was any good or not. Maybe a simple majority vote would do, and then I could open up a school.'

'I think we've covered that,' Comp said.

'A cat couldn't have done better,' Jackson agreed. 'Look, is there anyone else to talk to in this world except them and things like them?'

'Well, there is myself. I'm an inexhaustible conversationalist. I am also the definite didact. The number of things to be learned from me is finite, but very large. I assure you, if you choose it, that's a lifetime's occupation. A constantly expanding field of knowledge. Right at the moment, for example, the telemetry involved in sending exteroceptors across interstellar distances represents a fruitful – '

Jackson grinned, the way he had seen the Eld grin. 'And when you die, I can be you.'

'Heavens, no! I will never die!'

'That's what they all think,' Jackson sighed. 'What's Ahmuls doing?' He felt pretty lonely.

'Ahmuls is quite contented. Here . . .' Exteroaffectors kissed Jackson's eyelids.

At first, he thought what he saw was a runaway streamlet, tumbling, liquid and brown, swirling amidst stones. Then he realized it was an aerial view of a vast plain. The point of view dropped like a swooping hawk, and he plunged down towards a herd of tossing, shaggy brown animals, massive of head, high of shoulder, red-eyed, horned, and hairy. Extero-affectors nuzzled behind his ears, and he heard the thunder of the buffalo.

Behind them, bounding and lurching, came Ahmuls, silent, and purposeful. He ran in a way that told Jackson he was straining everything he had, but my God how he ran, his flesh bagging out behind him, away from his face and shoulders. His mouth was wide open, and the tip of his tongue was in the corner of his lips.

'This is the Mid-American Game Preserve,' Comp said. 'You'll notice the landscape has been slightly modified, to suit his special requirements.'

Indeed, the granite outcroppings that now split the herd into segments as it milled around them, and again flowed it into one cohesive mass before Ahmuls's pursuit startled it again, were covered with lichen. As he ran by one of them, Ahmuls threw out a hand, scooped off a clump, and stuffed it into his mouth. It was impossible to tell whether he was trying to catch the animals so he could kill them, or whether he was merely attempting to join them. But in the milling and stampeding, there were almost as many behind him as there were ahead, and once or twice panicked bulls clattering and snorting out of tight places between the rocks almost ran him down.

'What'll you do if he gets pounded flat?'

'Oh, there is no problem about that. He'd get medical attention immediately.'

'For the rest of his life.'

'That's my obligation. Accidental factors cannot be permitted to interrupt something's running its course.' Ahmuls disappeared from this particular exteroaffector's sight as he ran behind an outcropping. 'Do you want me to shift point of view, or do you want to look at Durstine now?'

Jackson opened his eyes, as he heard her say from in front of him: 'I wondered how long it would be before you came looking for me.'

It was hard shifting from the actuality to something he could see with his own eyes. It took a moment to organize his brain. He saw she was wearing some sort of crested helmet whose front part was a pale, sharp-edged mask over the upper part of her face, leaving only the chin and the red lips bare. Then he saw she was, in fact, gowned, unlike the decorated people inside. She stepped back, her body clad in swirling off-white gauzeries which might have been individual motes of pigment suspended in the air, or might even have been some wonderful fabric.

Either way it was some wonderful fabric, swirled around her body at the waist, caught again at the shoulders and the elbows. She laughed and sprang to tiptoe, her arms first out straight at the shoulders, then bent at the elbows to point towards him. The movement of her body scattered out her garment in lacy strands, upraised the crest of her mask, and flung wide her white wings. She laughed in a silvery tinkle of joy. 'See? I knew exactly what you wanted! I'm yours, yours!' she cried, throwing herself at him yieldingly.

He could just about get his hands up to catch her shoulders, and he felt himself wince when he touched them. 'You've got it just exactly backwards,' he said marvelling at their capacity. 'I got to admit, it's an accomplishment.'

'What? What?' She was jerking and tossing against his hands. 'What's the matter with you?'

'It's either you or me,' he admitted, swinging her around to push her backward through the doorway, trying to see to it she got where she belonged. Now what would Elmo Lincoln do in a case like this? 'Go. Go, mangani!' he burst out, pushing explosively, flinging her backward in a swirl and smother of garb. He was shaking with rage; he could hear Comp giggling.

He glared around him. There was nothing in sight but fake, and blue sky full of receptor glints. Never, never in his life had he been so angry, and Comp wouldn't stop giggling at him. He swatted at a darting bee. He wasn't as fast as Ahmuls.

He crouched, facing the doorway. Whoever came out of there first was in terrible trouble with him. He could see red mist edging his field of vision, and at the same time there was this terrible, wonderful clarity about how he felt. It was an excuse for anything. A man brought to this feeling was as much a monarch as Tyrannosaurus Rex had ever been. He prowled with his thighs flexed, his arms like bridge cable.

Pall came shyly and diffidently out of the Thorn tent. 'Don't be mad, Jackson,' she said. 'I know you're upset.' She stretched out her hand and touched his fist. 'I know how it is. They used to treat me that way. But I just learned to ignore it. And I didn't give up; I kept trying to improve myself, and one day . . .' Her eyes dropped. 'What you have to do,' she explained earnestly, 'is . . . well, learn to *express* yourself. Express *yourself*. You see, if you can only learn to trust in yourself, in what *you* are, if you feel confident in what you are, then . . . Well, you saw what happened. If you have confidence . . . and loving somebody can *give* you that confidence, or even just *admiring* them a lot can give you a lot of confidence . . . well, then, after that you can go along and do the same things everybody else does, and yet you're still expressing yourself, so you see, well, that's how you can be part of the group and still be yourself. I mean, knowing yourself lets you be part of a group. And you saw how they accepted me at last. Well, that's what makes it good because from now on, I'm going to always know that being part of a group is the only thing that lets you be yourself. And I can give you the same thing. Let me stay with you. I'll be good for you.'

Jackson looked up at the spiralling glints. 'You see that?' he asked. 'You hear?'

'Certainly. Would you like to see an actuality of Petra Jovans?'

Jackson shivered. 'No. Don't ever show me Petra Jovans.'

Pall was touching his hand to her mouth. 'Please, Jackson,'

she said, 'I really do understand you.'

Sweet Jesus, he thought. And then he thought, To me I am the only sane man conceivable. And she's just cuckoo enough to go along with it if I take her. 'Oh, come on,' he said, turning away from the tent, holding her wrist.

She trotted gracefully beside him. 'Where are we going?'

'I don't know.' He got them out between the pavilions and on to the fields. There was some kind of path out through the hedgerows, and he followed that. Exteroceptors were keeping pace with them.

'This is great stuff!' Comp was saying. 'Setting out for the New Eden! Man and his mate, on the endless journey to – '

'Horse shit,' Jackson said.

Pall stared at him. 'What was that for?'

What was it for? It always had to be for something, right? Jackson shook his head. 'You really want to know? You really want me to *express* myself, right?'

She nodded. 'Very much.'

All right. He began, 'The floor of the world is rippled like the bottom of the ocean, running out to the edges. Those edges are high and they're cruel. At sunset the eastern horizon is the far wall of the crater. It's black. Blue-black . . .'

'Great stuff! Marvellous!' Comp whispered admiringly in his ear. 'Forgive me. I thought all you were going to produce was some sort of cliché. Any cliché from you would be admirably dramatic, of course, with great and wide appeal. But I do not want you to think for a moment that I can't appreciate the raw, honest ring of visceral truth. The audience for it isn't so big, of course, but that's all right – it's good for them. Don't compromise. Don't soften it up just because you want to please *her*. Make it ring, boy! Tell it like it was!'

'. . . And thou beside me zinging in the wilderness,' Jackson muttered, Pall trotting along beside him with her eyes as bright as exteroceptors. Jackson said, 'The sunlight catches the top edge of the crater, and that's rust colour. It makes a long, rust-coloured arc that seems to dip down to left and right, like a wall, or a bow, or the trail of something that shot by without your noticing it, from one horizon to the other, and all you can see is the wake it left. There are rocks standing on the crater floor. The sunlight hitting them, just before it dies, turns them orange, too. The stars hang up there hard and sharp.

'That's the horizon you head for when you're honning Amsirs.

'In the beginning, I was chasing this bird . . .'

Explorations of the Marvellous Edited by Peter Nicholls

This isn't yet another promotional book by SF writers patting themselves – and each other – on the back. Consisting of eleven penetrating chapters – seven from writers inside the field (John Brunner, Philip K. Dick, Thomas M. Disch, Alan Garner, Harry Harrison, Ursula Le Guin and Robert Scheckley) and four from outside (psychologist Edward de Bono, critic Peter Nicholls, scientist John Taylor and futurologist Alvin Toffler) – it is a well informed, witty and sometimes sardonic account of where SF has been and where it is going, and the way it relates – and occasionally fails to relate – to the real world.

'An extremely rewarding, provocative book, streets ahead of similar compilations on what SF is all about' Ian Watson, author of *The Embedding, The Jonah Kit* and *The Martian Inca.*

'It is, in many respects, like the literature it describes: provocative and serious, yet simultaneously it is good entertainment' Christopher Priest, author of *Inverted World, The Space Machine* and *A Dream of Wessex*

The Grand Wheel Barrington Bayley

Cheyne Scarne was a gambler – a lucky one. What he didn't know about randomatics wasn't worth knowing. He had the brains to get right to the heart of the Grand Wheel – the syndicate that controlled all illegal activity in the planets under human control.

But what Scarne had staked to get that far was chicken feed compared to what he would risk to get into the real big time – the massive intergalactic combine that dwarfed the empires of mere men. For Scarne, double-crossing at every deal, had laid his life on the line to win a game where no one knew the value of the cards and the rules changed with every trick!

The Garments of Caean Barrington Bayley

In Caean, clothes weren't just for wearing – they were a whole philosophy of life. In the Ziode Cluster, though, things were different – Caeanic clothes were forbidden, their powers unrecognized, their scope unfulfilled.

But when Peder Forbarth looted a wrecked Caenic freighter and found the ultimate garment – the legendary Frachonard suit – he'd discovered something of unimaginable potential.

For the clothes didn't just make the man – they *were* the man! And Peder's new suit took him over, changed his character and set him off on a wild and spectacular odyssey across the galaxy.

But what had it done to the man inside?